Mallory and the Mystery Diary

**Look for these and other books
in the Baby-sitters Club series:**

Mallory and the Mystery Diary

Ann M. Martin

AN
APPLE
PAPERBACK

SCHOLASTIC INC.
New York Toronto London Auckland Sydney

For Mary Dietrich
and
Virginia Kilbourne,
who taught me to respect children

Cover art by Hodges Soileau

ISBN 0-590-42500-5

12 11 10 9 8 7 6 5 4 3 2 1   9/8 0 1 2 3 4/9

Printed in the U.S.A.   40

First Scholastic printing, November 1989

CHAPTER 1

If only I were thirteen instead of eleven. Life would be a picnic.

I closed my journal with a snap. I have been keeping a journal for some time now. The difference between a journal and a diary, as far as I can tell, is that a diary is a recording of daily events and you're supposed to write in it every day. For me, a diary entry would probably go like this (on a weekday):

Got up. Went to school. Made gum chains with Jessi during recess. Came home. Had a fight with Vanessa. Baby-sat for the Barrett kids. Went to a meeting of the Baby-sitters Club. Came home. Ate dinner. Had a fight with Mom over a pair of shoes I want that she won't let me buy. Did homework. Went to bed.

1

Pretty dull, huh? But a journal entry would be much more deep and sensitive and interesting. Also, I don't write in my journal every day, just whenever I feel like it. And my journal is a plain old composition book. You know, one of the ones with a mottled black-and-white cover. It's not set up with four lines for March 2nd, four lines for March 3rd, four lines for March 4th, etc. It's blank. So I can write as much or as little whenever I want. And I only write when I feel an urgency, which is often — whenever I'm angry or confused or think I haven't been treated fairly. Also when good things happen.

Yesterday I didn't write in my journal at all. Today, which is Sunday, I was feeling sort of pensive, so I wrote:

I feel as if I'm going to be eleven forever. My ninth year went by in a flash. My tenth year went by in a flash. But my eleventh year already seems a decade long. I think that's because I'm so anxious to be thirteen. I wonder if my twelfth year will seem a decade long, too. I hope not, because if it does, I'll feel thirty when I'm really only thirteen.

I hate my nose. I got it from my grandfather. I wish I could have a nose job, but my parents won't even let me get contacts so there's no hope for anything more drastic.

I wonder if other eleven-year-olds feel like this. If only I were thirteen instead of eleven. Life would be a picnic.

I hid my journal under my mattress. As far as I know, Vanessa hasn't found it there. It wouldn't be like her to go looking for it, though. Vanessa is a poet, and understands the need to keep your writing private.

Who's Vanessa? She's my sister. I have seven younger brothers and sisters in all. After me (I'm Mallory Pike) come the triplets — Byron, Adam, and Jordan. They're ten. Then there's Vanessa, who's nine; Nicky, who's eight; Margo, who's seven; and Claire, the baby of the family. Claire is five and very silly. She calls everybody a silly-billy-goo-goo. For instance, my Claire-name is Mallory-silly-billy-goo-goo.

Just as I was hiding my journal, I heard Mom call from downstairs, "Mal? Can you come here for a sec?"

"Sure," I replied. I patted the bed to be sure the mattress didn't look lumpy, and then dashed downstairs.

Mom was in the kitchen. She was wearing oven mitts and setting a casserole on a cooling rack.

"What's that?" I asked.

"It's a welcome-back present for Stacey and Mrs. McGill. I know they moved in a week ago, but I figure a casserole is always appreciated. They've been unpacking for a week, Mrs. McGill has been looking for a job, and Stacey's been busy with school and the Baby-sitters Club. I know they haven't had much time for cooking. If they don't want to eat this now, they can freeze it and have it some other night."

"Gosh, that's awfully nice of you, Mom," I said. "I know the McGills will appreciate it."

"Do you mind taking it over?" she asked me.

"Of course not. I'd love to see Stacey."

"Great. Just give it about fifteen minutes to cool off a little."

"Okay," I replied.

You may be wondering who Stacey and her mom are — and also what the Baby-sitters Club (the BSC) is. Well, while Mom's casserole

4

cools, I'll tell you about the McGills and my BSC friends.

First of all, the BSC is a club that I belong to. It's really more of a business, and the other people in it are my friends Jessi Ramsey, Stacey McGill, Kristy Thomas, Dawn Schafer, Mary Anne Spier, and Claudia Kishi. What our club does is baby-sit for families here in Stoneybrook, Connecticut. It is super-fun, and I feel very cool to be allowed in it.

You see, the club was started by Kristy, Claudia, Stacey, and Mary Anne, who are all thirteen years old now and in eighth grade. Jessi and I are the only eleven-year-old sixth-graders. I am so glad the club is back together again. For quite awhile, we had to make do without Stacey. In fact, Kristy (she's the club president) asked Jessi and me to join when Stacey's family moved from Stoneybrook back to New York City, which was where they'd come from in the first place. (They'd moved both times because Mr. McGill's company kept transferring him.) Then, after they moved back to New York, Mr. and Mrs. McGill decided to get divorced. They'd been having problems for awhile. So Mr. McGill stayed in New York with his job, and Mrs. McGill and Stacey returned to Stoneybrook. Unfortunately, they couldn't move into their old house. Guess why? Jessi Ramsey's family had moved into it! But Stacey and her mom found a nice old house that they like — and it's right behind ours. It there weren't so many trees in the way, I'd be able to look out our back windows and into Stacey's back windows. Maybe that will happen when the trees are bare. At any rate, it's nice to be able to walk out our back door, through our backyard, and right into Stacey's backyard.

On the day that Mom fixed the casserole, the McGills had been back for a week and a day. That meant that Stacey had been to three BSC meetings since her return — and, boy, were the rest of us glad to have her back.

I guess I should tell you a little about the girls in the BSC, since the club is basically the most important thing in my life. First, there's Kristy Thomas. I'm starting with her because she's the president of the club. She dreamed it up and got it going. Kristy is part of an interesting family. She has two older brothers, Sam and Charlie, who are in high school, and one much younger brother, David Michael. He's seven. Kristy's parents are divorced. They got divorced a long time ago and Kristy never sees her father. However, last summer her mother married this millionaire, Watson Brewer, who whisked the Thomases across town to his mansion. (Kristy used to live on Bradford Court, next to her best friend, Mary Anne Spier, and across the street from Claudia Kishi. But not anymore.) Watson has two little kids, Karen and Andrew, who are six and four. They're from his first marriage and live at the Brewer mansion every other weekend. (The rest of the time they live with their mother.) Kristy adores them. It's a full household — and even fuller since Nannie, Kristy's grandmother, moved in to help run the house after the Brewers adopted Emily Michelle, a two-year-old Vietnamese girl.

Kristy is brown-haired, brown-eyed, the shortest kid in her class, and doesn't care a bit about clothes. She always wears jeans, running shoes, a turtleneck, and a sweater (well, not in the middle of summer, of course). She has a big mouth, which sometimes gets her in trouble, she can be bossy, and she's a tomboy. She loves sports. She's also *great* with children, and coaches a softball team for little kids called Kristy's Krushers. I used to be intimidated by Kristy, but now I like her.

The vice-president of the BSC is Claudia Kishi. Claud is one terrific person. She's a really talented artist and she knows how to paint, sculpt, make jewelry, sketch, draw, and do other things. She's a total junk-food nut and keeps candy and stuff hidden all over her room. (She has to hide it since her parents do not approve of this habit.) Claud is also one of the coolest dressers I know. She would never, ever get arrested by the Fashion Police. She wears long, baggy sweaters, tight leggings, dresses with flared skirts, little ballet slippers, and wild jewelry. She makes a lot of the jewelry herself. To top things off, she is gorgeous. She's Japanese-American, and has LONG, silky, jet-black hair; a creamy, perfect complexion; and dark, almond-shaped eyes.

The one unfortunate thing about Claud is that even though she's smart, she's a terrible student. Her older sister, Janine, on the other hand, is an actual genius. Claud reads Nancy Drew books; Janine studies stuff like biogenetics and physics. Claudia and Janine live with their parents. Until recently, Claud's beloved grandmother, Mimi, lived with them, too, but Mimi died not long ago. That's been tough on Claudia.

Stacey McGill is the BSC's treasurer. I know her parents' divorce has been hard on her, but she does a pretty good job of covering up her feelings, I guess, because so far she has seemed like the old Stace to me. Stacey and Claudia are best friends, and no wonder. They share the same wild taste in clothes and are pretty sophisticated for thirteen, although neither of them has a steady boyfriend. Stacey has blue eyes and short, fluffy, blonde hair, which is often permed. She's a pretty good student, especially in math, which is why she's our treasurer, but she has one big problem (I mean, apart from the divorce). Stacey has diabetes. Actually, she's fine as long as she sticks to her diet and gives herself daily insulin shots. But who wants to keep track of calories all day, avoid sugar and sweets, and give herself injections? Not me. Stacey is philosophical, though. She says she'd rather do those things than get sick.

Stacey is an only child, and I guess from now on she'll be spending vacations and certain weekends with her father in New York. Her parents have said she can live with whichever one of them she wants, whenever she wants, just as long as the back-and-forth doesn't interfere with her schoolwork.

Our club secretary is Mary Anne Spier. Mary

Anne and Kristy grew up together and are best friends (although Mary Anne has another best friend — Dawn Schafer). Mary Anne is like Kristy in that she is short and also has brown hair and brown eyes, and neither of them is as sophisticated as Stacey or Claudia. But there are major differences between Kristy and Stacey. For starters, Mary Anne's family is as simple as Kristy's is complicated. Mary Anne lives with just her dad and her kitten, Tigger. Her mom died so long ago that Mary Anne barely remembers her. When Mr. Spier found himself raising a daughter alone, he decided that the best way to do that would be very strictly. He invented a million rules for Mary Anne about what she could wear, what she could do, and where she could go. Now that Mary Anne's growing up, though, he's relaxed his rules — and two things happened right away. One, Mary Anne began choosing her own clothes, and they are much trendier. Two, she became the first one of us to have a steady boyfriend. His name is Logan Bruno and he's *really* nice. I think Mary Anne was *meant* to have a boyfriend. She's extremely romantic, very sensitive (actually, she cries a lot), a good listener, and patient and quiet. How she and loudmouth Kristy have remained friends for so long is beyond me. Anyway, Mary Anne is a wonderful person.

Dawn Schafer is the club's alternate officer. (I'll explain what that means later.) Dawn has had a difficult year or so. Like Stacey, her parents got divorced. But her mom moved Dawn and her brother, Jeff, all the way from California to Connecticut. That's because Mrs. Schafer grew up here and her parents still live in Stoneybrook. Dawn likes Connecticut okay, and she likes being near her grandparents, but she's a California girl at heart and misses it badly. Her brother missed it so much that he finally moved back there to live with his father, so now Dawn's family is cracked in two. But Dawn copes well.

Dawn is an individual. She's never rude, but she always does what she pleases. She stands up for what she believes in, dresses the way she likes (we call her style California casual), and eats health food while the rest of us pig out on junk food and red meat.

Dawn has the L-O-N-G-E-S-T, blondest hair I've ever seen (it's almost white), and sparkly bright blue eyes. Here's an interesting fact about her. She lives in a very old farmhouse with a *secret passage*, and that passage just might be haunted by the ghost of a long-ago crazy man named Jared Mullray. This is okay with Dawn since she *loves* ghost stories, true or made up.

Well, the only two club members left are Jessi and me. We're junior officers, and are very much alike except for two things. I come from a huge family and Jessi comes from a normal-sized one. And I'm white and Jessi is black. These differences haven't affected us much, though. We are the best of friends. We're both eleven and the oldest in our families, we both feel that our parents treat us like babies, we both love to baby-sit (of course), and we both like to read, especially horse stories by Marguerite Henry. Beyond that, our interests are different. I like to write and draw, and I'm thinking of becoming an author and illustrator of children's books. Jessi, though, is an amazing ballet dancer. She's taken lessons for years, and attends a fancy ballet school in Stamford, Connecticut, which isn't too far away. She has danced on stage before big audiences. She dances on toe, or as Jessi says, *en pointe*.

In Jessi's family are her parents, her shy eight-year-old sister, Becca, and her baby brother, Squirt. Squirt's real name is John Philip Ramsey, Jr., but when he was born, he was so tiny that the nurses in the hospital nicknamed him Squirt. I wish I could say that the Ramseys had an easy time moving to Stoneybrook earlier this year, but they didn't. They're one of the few black families in town — and Jessi is the only black student in the whole sixth grade. I'm ashamed to say that some people were not very nice to them at first, but things have gotten better for the Ramseys.

"Mallory!" my mother called then. "I think you can take the casserole over to Stacey's now."

"Okay," I replied.

It was time to quit my daydreaming and get moving.

CHAPTER 2

Mom's casserole wasn't boiling anymore, but it was still pretty hot, so I had to carry it over to the McGills' with oven mitts.

Claire held our back door open for me.

"Thank you," I said.

"You're welcome, Mallory-silly-billy-goo-goo. . . . Can I come with you?"

I thought about that. Claire loves Stacey, and I would need someone to ring the McGills' bell for me. On the other hand, if I stayed at the McGills', I didn't really want Claire hanging around.

At last I said tactfully, "I think the McGills are still unpacking, Claire. Their house is probably a mess. You know, boxes everywhere. I bet Stacey would rather have you see her house when it's all fixed up."

Claire accepted that. "Okay," she said. "Tell

Stacey I love her. Tell her she's still a silly-billy-goo-goo."

I grinned. "All right. See you later, alligator."

"After awhile, crocodile."

Sometimes, like now, Claire can be absolutely wonderful. At other times she can be a pain . . . in . . . the . . . NECK!

I walked carefully through our backyard, through Stacey's backyard, and around to the front of her house. I climbed her porch steps and stood at the door. Now — how was I supposed to ring the bell? The casserole weighed a ton and I needed both hands to carry it. I tried resting it on my leg long enough to let go with one hand, but — "OW!" The casserole wasn't nearly cooled off. I was about to set it on the porch floor when I heard someone call, "Hello?"

"Hi . . . Stace? It's me, Mallory."

The front door opened. "I thought I heard someone out here," she said, grinning. "Come on in."

"Thanks." I stepped inside. "This is for you and your mom. My mother made it. It's a tuna casserole. And it's burning hot and incredibly heavy."

Stacey hurried me into the kitchen, where I set the casserole on the stove.

"Gosh, that was nice of your mother," said Stacey. "We've been eating take-out food all week, except for Thursday night when the Kishis invited us over for dinner. . . . Mom?" she called. "Hey, Mom!"

Mrs. McGill appeared from somewhere, looking dusty.

"Hi, Mal," she greeted me.

"Hi," I replied.

"Mom, look what Mrs. Pike sent over. A tuna casserole."

"Oh, how nice!" Stacey's mother lifted the lid off the dish and breathed in deeply. "Oh, that smells wonderful!" she exclaimed. "I'll call your mother to thank her as soon as I have a spare moment."

"You want to stay for awhile?" Stacey asked me. "Claud's here. She's helping Mom and me. Believe it or not, we're pretty much unpacked. But there are cartons and crumpled-up newspapers and those little Styrofoam things everywhere. So now we're trying to clean up. Claud's in the living room. Come take a look around."

It was funny. I'd always lived behind the

house Stacey had moved into, but I'd never been inside it. So I was pretty eager to look around, especially since it was such an old house.

Stacey took me on a tour. "This is the dining room. And this is the back hall. See? Those steps go upstairs, and there's another set of stairs at the front of the house."

"Cool!" I said.

Stacey led me all around the first floor and I looked at the low doorways, the funny wavy panes of glass in the windows, and the floors that tilted a little.

We met up with Claud and Mrs. McGill in the living room. Claudia was stuffing newspaper and Styrofoam bits into big garbage bags.

"I think we should save the boxes, though," Mrs. McGill said.

"Are you kidding?" said Stacey. "You *better* save them — after all the trouble I went through collecting those things in New York!" She turned to me. "I had to go begging at the grocery store nearly every day while we were packing. I thought the manager was going to kill me. There's no way I'm throwing them out."

"Why don't you take them up to the attic?" suggested Mrs. McGill. "We can always use boxes."

"The attic?" repeated Stacey. "I don't even know where it is. It's not one of those ladders you have to pull down from the ceiling, is it?"

"No. It's that doorway next to your bathroom, upstairs."

"You're kidding. I thought that was a linen closet. I didn't even bother to look inside!"

"That's because you hate changing your sheets," said Mrs. McGill, and we laughed.

Claud, Stacey, and I each nested some boxes together. We climbed to the second floor with them. Then Stacey opened the door to the "linen closet."

"What do you know?" she said. She put her boxes down and groped for a switch plate. "I am *not* going up these stairs in the dark," she announced.

"What are you afraid of? Bogeymen?" asked Claudia.

"Yes," replied Stacey. "We didn't have bogeymen in New York."

Stacey found the switch then, turned on the light, and we climbed the stairs cautiously.

"Phew, is it ever dusty here," said Claud.

"Really," I agreed, and sneezed.

18

We reached the top of the stairs, put our boxes on the floor, and just stared.

"Whoa," said Stacey. "Would you look at this."

Claudia and I were speechless. The attic was small, but it was crammed with stuff. I saw an old rocking chair, a brass headboard for a bed, several stacks of old magazines, a bird cage, a box full of books, one of those big, dome-shaped radios, a huge trunk, and more.

"I wonder who all this belongs to," Stacey whispered, and shivered. "Not the last people who owned the house. It looks like it's been around forever. Anyway, why wouldn't they have taken it with them?"

"An awful lot of people have lived in this house," I pointed out. "If every family left a few things behind, then — " I swept my hand around as if to say, "Well, you see what can happen."

Stacey took a step forward and tripped over one of our stacks of boxes. "Sheesh! There's barely room for these. But we'd have a lot more space if we got rid of that." She pointed to the trunk.

"Got *rid* of *that?!*" I cried. The trunk was handsome. Dusty, but handsome. Its lid was rounded. It was made of a rich-colored leather, and the fastenings were brass. "You can't get rid of it! It's beautiful!" I exclaimed. "Besides, think what might be in it."

I crossed the attic, stepping over the boxes, and reached the trunk. I tried to open it. "Uh-oh," I said. "It's locked." I tried to lift it. I couldn't get it even an inch off the floor. "It must be stuffed," I added.

"I wonder what *is* in it," said Claud, joining me. Her eyes had sort of glazed over. I knew she was thinking of Nancy Drew and mysteries.

"Girls?" called Stacey's mother then. "What are you doing up there?"

"Come see what we found," Stacey yelled down the stairs.

Mrs. McGill, sneezing, climbed the stairs to the attic. "Goodness, it's crowded up here!" she exclaimed.

Then Stacey showed her the trunk. "It *is* pretty," she said to her mother, mostly, I think, so as not to insult Claud and me, "but it's taking up way too much space. And it's locked, so we can't even see what's in it."

"It is taking up an awful lot of space," Mrs. McGill agreed. "We should probably just throw it away. We'll put it out for the garbage collector."

20

"No!" cried Claudia and I at the same time.

"Nancy Drew and Miss Marple want to see what's in the trunk," Stacey informed her mother.

"Well, you're welcome to have it," said Mrs. McGill.

Claud and I looked at each other. How would we decide who got the trunk?

Claud solved the problem. "You take it, Mal," she said. "My room's a crowded mess already. Besides, it'll be easier to get the trunk to your house. You live much closer by."

So I called the triplets and they agreed to lug the trunk out of the attic, down the stairs, through the yards to our house, and up to the room I share with Vanessa.

I had to pay them a dollar each, but it was worth it.

When the trunk had been unloaded in my bedroom, Vanessa just stared at it. "Where did that come from?" she asked.

I told her the story.

"And where are we going to put it?" she wanted to know.

"At the foot of my bed." I managed to shove it over.

Vanessa grinned. "Okay. Now let's open it."

"Can't," I told her. "It's locked."

"Locked!" Vanessa sounded angry, but then this poetic look came over her face. "I think," she said dramatically, "that I shall write about a mystery trunk." Vanessa grabbed for pencil and paper, a poem already forming in her mind.

But all I could do was stare at the beautiful trunk. I was sure it held secrets.

CHAPTER 3

The next day, Monday, I ran straight home after school, eager to look at my trunk.

It was still unopened.

The evening before, the triplets had begged me to break the locks so we could get inside it, but I wouldn't let them. I wanted the trunk opened, too, but I didn't want to ruin it.

"Try bobby pins," suggested Adam. "They always work in the movies." So we did, but nothing happened.

"Try a credit card," suggested Byron. "That works, too."

His brothers gave him withering looks. "It doesn't work on *trunks*," they informed him. "It works on doors to people's houses."

"How about a coat hanger!" cried Vanessa.

That drew more withering looks.

"Coat hangers," said Jordan, "are for getting into your car when you've locked yourself out."

"Isn't there a key somewhere?" asked Nicky, joining us in the bedroom.

I shook my head. "Nope. Stacey and I searched the attic."

"Maybe it's taped to the bottom of the trunk or something," said Vanessa.

The six of us searched every inch of the trunk.

No key.

"Well," I said. "That's that. At least for now. I'll think more about this tomorrow."

Monday afternoon arrived and I didn't have any new ideas. I could tell that the locked trunk was driving Vanessa crazy. She was writing poems like a demon, and casting long, soulful glances at both the trunk and me.

Finally she said, "I bet you could smash those locks with a hammer."

"No way," I replied. "That would ruin the trunk."

I was glad when it was time to leave for a BSC meeting. I wouldn't have to watch the tortured poet anymore.

Our club meetings are held from five-thirty until six every Monday, Wednesday, and Fri-

24

day afternoon. I like to get to club headquarters (Claudia's bedroom) a little before five-thirty. If you are even a speck late, Kristy starts the meeting without you.

So I was pleased to enter headquarters at 5:25 that day. When I did, I found Claudia, Kristy, and Mary Anne already there. Claud was fishing around on the shelf of her closet, probably looking for junk food. Mary Anne was seated on Claudia's bed, reading the club notebook (I'll explain about that in a minute), and Kristy was in her official presidential position — sitting in Claud's director's chair, wearing a visor, a pencil stuck over one ear. She insists that our meetings — that the club itself — be run in as businesslike a way as possible.

This must be a good tactic, since the club is so successful. Let me tell you how it began, and how we run it.

As I said before, the club was Kristy's idea. It came to her one day when her mom needed a sitter for David Michael, and neither Kristy nor one of her big brothers was available. So Mrs. Thomas started making phone calls. She made call after call, and while she did so, Kristy was thinking, Wouldn't it save time if her mother could make one call and reach a lot of baby-sitters at once, instead of calling one person after another?

So she got together with Mary Anne and Claudia, who were her neighbors then (they'd grown up together), and the three of them decided to start a club to baby-sit in their neighborhood. They also decided that they needed a fourth member, so they asked Stacey to join. Stacey had just moved to Stoneybrook (for the first time) and was a new friend of Claud's.

The club was a huge success. Soon they needed a fifth member and invited Dawn, who was getting to be friends with Mary Anne, to join. Then when Stacey had to go back to New York, the other girls asked Jessi and me to take her place.

How does the club run? Well, thanks to advertising (a little ad in the Stoneybrook newspaper and a lot of fliers in mailboxes), people around here know when we meet and call us during those times to line up sitters. When one of us answers Claud's phone, that person takes down all the information about the job. Then Mary Anne checks our schedule to see who's free, and we call the client back to tell her (or him) who the sitter will be.

Each of us has a special job to do in order

to keep the club operating smoothly.

Kristy's job as president is to come up with new ideas for the club, to run the meetings, and to solve problems.

Claudia, our vice-president, doesn't actually have a *job*, but because she's the only one of us with her own phone and private phone number, we meet in her room so that we don't have to tie up our parents' lines. Since we invade her room three times a week, we think it's only fair that she be the VP.

Mary Anne is the secretary and has the biggest, most complicated job of all of us. She is in charge of the club record book (not to be confused with the club notebook). The record book is where all important club information is written down — our clients' names, addresses, and phone numbers; special information about the kids we sit for; and most important of all, our schedules. Mary Anne has to keep track of Jessi's ballet classes, Claudia's art lessons, my orthodontist appointments (did I mention my disgusting braces?), and other things like that, in order to know who's free when, so she can safely schedule sitting jobs for us. She has never once made a mistake.

Stacey is the treasurer, in charge of collecting our weekly dues every Monday and keeping an eye on the money in our treasury. We use that money for several things. One is for fun club stuff. Since we work so hard we like to treat ourselves to sleepovers or pizza parties every now and then. Another is to pay Kristy's older brother Charlie to drive her to and from meetings since she lives so far away now. The third is to buy new items for our Kid-Kits. Kid-Kits were one of Kristy's big ideas. We've each got a cardboard box that is decorated with fabric and paint and stuff, and filled with our old toys, books, and games. We take our Kid-Kits along sometimes when we baby-sit, and the children love them! But things get used up, and every now and then we have to buy new crayons or a coloring book or sticker book.

Dawn is our alternate officer, meaning that she can take over the job of any officer who might be absent from a meeting. She's kind of like a substitute teacher. It's a hard job because she has to know what *everyone* does. (When Stacey was back in New York, Dawn became the treasurer, but now that Stacey has returned, Dawn gladly took over her old job. She isn't wild about math, and Stacey is.)

Jessi and I are junior officers. To be honest, we don't have jobs. "Junior officer" simply means that since we're eleven we're only allowed to sit during the daytime — not at night unless we're sitting for our own brothers and sisters. But we don't mind. We get plenty of after-school and weekend jobs.

Two more things about the club, just to show you how officially Kristy runs it. One, she makes us keep a club notebook. In the notebook, each of us is responsible for writing up every single job we go on. Then we're supposed to read the book once a week to see what's happened while our friends were sitting. We learn how they handled problems with kids and things like that. I think everyone but Kristy and me hates writing in the notebook. I like it just because I enjoy writing, and Kristy *has* to like it, since the notebook was her idea. Two, our club has a couple of associate members. They don't come to meetings, but they're good sitters whom we can call on if a job is offered to the club that no one else can take. One of our associates is a friend of Kristy's named Shannon Kilbourne. The other is none other than . . . Logan Bruno, Mary Anne's boyfriend!

Well, I think that's everything you need to know about the running of the club.

* * *

By five-thirty, the seven of us had gathered in Claud's room and were eating pretzels. (Pretzels are one snack food that Stacey can eat and Dawn doesn't consider too junky.) Kristy had opened the meeting and we were waiting for the phone to ring.

"Did you get the trunk unlocked?" Stacey asked me while we waited.

"No, darn it," I replied, and then she and Claud and I had to explain about the trunk.

"We can't find a key, and bobby pins don't work," I added.

"Did you try dynamite?" asked Kristy.

We laughed.

We were still laughing when the first job call came in. For a few moments, no one could calm down. At last Stacey composed herself, picked up the phone, turned toward the wall so she wouldn't have to look at us, and spoke to Mrs. Barrett, who has three little kids. The Barretts live near Dawn and me.

Mary Anne checked the schedule and the job was given to Dawn.

Then Kristy said, "Okay, we have to *settle down*. We have to *be businesslike*."

So we did settle down. But every time I thought about blasting the trunk open with dynamite, I wanted to start giggling again.

CHAPTER 4

Tuesday

Uh-oh. There hasn't been much trouble in the Barrett household lately, but there was today. Buddy's teacher had sent home a note saying that his reading is "below grade level." Well, that set off all sorts of problems. Mrs. Barrett was upset, but not with Buddy. She was upset with herself, I think, for not being able to spend extra time with him on his reading. Buddy was upset too, of course, and when Suzi tried to show off... disaster!

Wow. Dawn *used* to have disastrous days with the Barrett kids. She called them the Impossible Three. The Impossible Three are Buddy, who is eight and in third grade, Suzi, who is five and in kindergarten, and Marnie, who's just two. Only they're not so impossible anymore.

The reason they used to be impossible was that Mr. and Mrs. Barrett has just gotten a divorce and Mrs. Barrett was not used to coping with three little kids by herself, running a household, and looking for a job. But now she's found a part-time job — a good one — and is much more organized. So things have been going better for the Barretts. I was hoping that Buddy's reading problem was just a small setback.

Anyway, Dawn rang the Barretts' bell five minutes before Mrs. Barrett had asked her to arrive. Us baby-sitters have found that getting to a job a little early is a good idea. (Of course, if you can't get there early, definitely be right on time.) But arriving early gives the parent, or parents, a few extra moments for explanations or to say a special good-bye to the kids. The sitting job starts off in a more relaxed way.

Usually.

Dawn's job wouldn't have started off well no matter when she'd arrived. That was because she walked into a crisis.

The doorbell was answered by Suzi, who whispered dramatically to Dawn, "Fight! In the kitchen! Buddy did something bad!"

Oh, no, thought Dawn, as she went inside. She was greeted by the sound of Buddy saying, "I *do* try. I *don't* fool around in class."

"But honey — " Mrs. Barrett began.

"Mom," interrupted Buddy, "I'm a good enough reader to read most of Mr. Moser's note. And he says you should help me at home."

"I know he does. I just don't know when we can — Oh, hi, Dawn." Mrs. Barrett paused as Dawn entered the kitchen.

"Hi," Dawn replied, feeling embarrassed. "Do — do you want me to take Suzi outside or something?"

"No, no. That's all right. You don't have to leave. We've just got a little problem. Buddy's teacher has suggested that I try to spend some 'quality time' with him in order to improve his reading. You know, flash cards, reading aloud, that sort of thing. But I've got three kids and only so much 'quality time.' I don't see any way to stretch that time."

"I don't want flash cards anyway," mumbled Buddy. "Besides, I can read."

"I know you can read," said Mrs. Barrett wearily. "Mr. Moser is just saying that you don't read quite as well as the other kids in your class."

"So what?" countered Buddy crossly. He was sitting at the kitchen table, kicking the legs of his chair with his heels.

"*I* can read," spoke up Suzi importantly. "I can read lots of words. We're learning in kindergarten."

Buddy threw his sister a murderous glance.

Mrs. Barrett didn't seem to notice any of this. Instead she said, "I don't think Mr. Moser knows what he's asking. I work at home in the mornings so that I don't have to pay for a sitter for Marnie. Then I go to the office most afternoons and some evenings. When I'm not working, I'm trying to cook, clean, and play with each of the children. How am I supposed to be a reading teacher, too?"

Dawn felt pretty bad for Mrs. Barrett and Buddy, but she wasn't sure what to say. It didn't matter. Mrs. Barrett flew off to work in her usual rush then, saying, "Marnie's napping but she should be up soon. Buddy and Suzi have just had juice and cookies, so no more snacks. Marnie can have some milk when she gets up, though. Her special cup is on the counter." She quickly kissed Buddy and Suzi. Then she was gone.

"Okay, you guys, what do you want to do today?" asked Dawn. "It's getting sort of drizzly out, so we better stay indoors."

Before the kids could answer, Dawn heard Marnie upstairs. "Mommy, Mommy, Mommy!" she was singing.

"I better go get Marnie," said Dawn. "I'm sure she'll need to be changed, so I'll be a few minutes. Why don't you two play with Pow in the rec room?" (Pow is the Barretts' basset hound.)

Buddy and Suzi obediently headed for the stairs to the rec room, but Buddy looked like he'd just lost his best friend. Dawn paused, thinking, then dashed upstairs to Marnie.

"Hi, Marnie-O," she greeted her.

Marnie was standing in her crib. She was surprised to see Dawn instead of her mother, and for just a moment her lower lip quivered.

Dawn pretended nothing was wrong. She sang "Baa, Baa, Black Sheep" very softly, pulled up the window shade, and straightened the things on Marnie's changing table. By the time she turned back to the crib, Marnie was smiling. She likes Dawn.

Dawn picked Marnie up, laid her on the changing table, and said in a low voice, "Do you want me to . . . tickle, tickle?"

"No! No!" shrieked Marnie, laughing.

Then Dawn played peek-a-boo with Marnie, changed her diaper, took her down to the kitchen, and gave her some milk in her two-handled cup.

"Dawn?" called Buddy from the rec room.

"Yes?" Dawn replied. She was putting the milk carton back in the refrigerator.

"Suzi's bothering me."

"Am not!" cried Suzi indignantly.

"Are too!"

"Am not!"

"Are too!"

"Can it, you guys," Dawn called. "Marnie and I will be there in a minute. Just as soon as she finishes her milk." (We have all learned that it is not a good idea to let Marnie eat or drink anything in a room with a rug on the floor.)

When Marnie's cup was empty, Dawn led her downstairs (a slow process). She was greeted by the sight of Buddy and Suzi sitting scrunched up at opposite ends of the couch, purposefully ignoring each other. Their heads were turned away from one another and their arms were crossed.

"All right," said Dawn. "I don't know what's going on, but stop it. Suzi, would you like to be my big helper today?"

"Sure!"

"Good. Why don't you and Marnie build something with blocks. I'm going to give Buddy a hand with his reading."

"You are?" said Buddy in astonishment.

"Yup."

"Do you promise — no flash cards?"

"Cross my heart," replied Dawn solemnly.

"Well . . . okay."

Suzi and Marnie settled themselves at one end of the rec room. They dumped out a big carton of wooden blocks and turned *Sesame Street* on low. At the other end of the room, Dawn sat Buddy next to her. She held a copy of *Green Eggs and Ham* in her lap.

"Here," she said to Buddy. "Try reading this."

Buddy made a face but opened the book to the first page. " 'I . . . am . . . same,' " he read slowly.

"No, no," interrupted Dawn. "Not 'same.' It's 'Sam.' See? It's that funny guy's name."

Buddy nodded. He turned the page. The words were repeated. " 'I . . . am . . . Sa — Sam,' " he corrected himself.

"Good!" exclaimed Dawn.

Next page. " 'Sam . . . I am.' "

"Great!"

Next page. Nothing. Buddy didn't open his mouth.

"Go ahead," said Dawn.

"No. This is too hard."

"Okay, I'll read a few pages." Dawn read up to page nineteen. Then she gave the book back to Buddy. "Now you try again."

" 'Wuh-wuh — ' "

"Would," supplied Dawn.

" 'Would . . . you like . . . them . . . in a . . .' "

Buddy paused.

"House!" cried Suzi. She had crept to the couch and was peering over Buddy's shoulder. "I know that word. We learned it in kindergarten. And that word is 'mouse'!"

With that, Buddy slammed the book shut. He stuffed it between the cushions of the couch. "I hate this old book anyway," he announced. "It's for babies and it's boring."

"It is not for babies!" squawked Suzi, insulted.

"Yes, it is."

"Okay, okay," said Dawn. "Enough reading. And enough fighting," she added. "Suzi, you go help Marnie again. Buddy, the rain has stopped. Why don't you take Pow out in the backyard and give him some exercise?"

Dawn knew Buddy needed to escape. She also knew he needed help — lots of it — with his reading. And by the time Mrs. Barrett came home, she had an idea.

She waited until she was alone at the front door with Buddy's mother. Then she said, "I was reading a little with Buddy today and I think he *is* having some problems. I was just wondering — would you like somebody in the Baby-sitters Club to tutor Buddy? I mean, spend a few hours a week working alone with him? Maybe he just needs some special attention."

"Oh, Dawn, that would be wonderful. You're a lifesaver. As always," said Mrs. Barrett.

Dawn grinned. "I'll have to wait until our next club meeting so we can see who could fit something like that into her schedule. I'll call you tomorrow, okay?"

"Okay!" Mrs. Barrett looked very relieved, and Dawn felt quite proud of herself.

CHAPTER 5

Monday and Tuesday had passed. So had Wednesday and Thursday. Now, on Friday afternoon, we still hadn't opened the trunk. It was another drizzly day. I had nothing to do until our BSC meeting at five-thirty. Vanessa and I were sitting on my bed, staring at the trunk. We were on my bed because Vanessa's was littered with half-finished poems and there was no room for her.

Suddenly Vanessa jumped up and cried, "I can't stand it any longer! That trunk is driving me crazy. We've got to open it. Now!"

"But we can't," I replied. "We've tried everything. And I *don't* want to break it."

"So you're going to let it sit here locked up forever, and never get to see what's in it?"

That did seem sort of silly. But all I said was, "I don't want to ruin it."

Vanessa looked thoughtful. Then she said, "If you do not open that trunk, then I will be in a big, bad funk."

"Are you going to start talking in rhymes again?" I asked warily.

"Probably."

I ran to our doorway. "Byron! Jordan! Adam! Come quick! And bring a hammer and a wrench!"

I absolutely cannot stand it when Vanessa speaks in rhymes. I'd do anything to prevent it. Even break the locks on the beautiful trunk.

A few moments later the triplets arrived with the tools.

"What is it?" asked Adam. "What are you doing?"

I pointed to the trunk. "Open it," I commanded. "Break the locks."

"All *right!*" exclaimed Jordan.

The boys attacked the locks. I squinched my eyes shut. I couldn't bear to look. I heard pounding and smashing and grunting. I heard Byron say, "I'll go get the crowbar." (Oh, no. Not that, I thought.) At last I heard a *skreek*, and Vanessa cried, "It's open! It's open!"

I dared to peek. The trunk was in better shape than I'd expected. Except for the fact that the locks were just barely hanging onto the lid, the trunk looked okay.

Vanessa was already digging into it.

"Look! Look!" she was crying. "Clothes! They're . . . they're gorgeous. I bet they're antiques."

"Be careful with them, then," I said. I peered into the trunk. I saw mounds of old, white, lacy petticoats and dresses and blouses. They were all handsewn. And Vanessa was right. They were probably antiques. "They look awfully fragile," I added.

Vanessa nodded. She was already handling them more delicately.

"Thanks, you g — " I started to say to the triplets, but they were heading down the hall, muttering things like, "Boring," and, "All that work for a bunch of old clothes."

Vanessa and I carefully lifted the clothes out of the trunk, one by one. We hadn't even finished when Vanessa began trying things on. Most of the clothes were in girls' sizes. But I kept emptying the trunk. I had a funny feeling that something else would be in it besides clothes.

I almost decided I was wrong, though: I didn't find the diary until I'd reached the very bottom of the trunk.

"Ooh," I said under my breath. "Look at this." But Vanessa was too busy looking at herself in the mirror.

I sat on the edge of my bed and opened the diary. The first page read, "This is my book, by Sophie. And this is a year in my life — 1894."

"Eighteen ninety-four," I said, awed. "That's ages and ages ago."

"Huh?" said Vanessa, but I could tell she wasn't really interested.

I turned to the next page. It was headed *January 1, 1894*. Underneath was a whole page in Sophie's handwriting. It wasn't easy to read. She made her letters oddly — all sprawled out, she wasn't the world's best speller, and the ink was faded. But of course I began reading right away. I didn't even feel guilty. I would have felt *horribly* guilty sneaking a peek at a friend's diary, but Sophie said on the first page that she was twelve years old, so I figured she wasn't alive anymore. If she were, she'd be over a hundred. This wasn't prying — it was history.

As I read, I thought how lucky I was. I mean, just to be reading. When you read, you can sit in your room and travel back and forth in time, or to other countries, or to made-up lands, or to outer space. And all without moving a muscle, except to turn pages. I thought about Buddy Barrett. It was going to be my job to help turn him into a reader. I was going to be his tutor. Mrs. Barrett and I had agreed that we would try a few sessions (Tuesdays and Thursdays from four until six) to see how things went.

I wanted them to go well. I wanted Buddy to like reading as much as I did.

"How do I look?" spoke up Vanessa. She turned away from the mirror. She was completely dressed in white — with a lot of lace. She was wearing a white dress over two white petticoats. On her hands were white lace gloves. But on her feet were black shoes with about a million buttons on them.

"Where did those come from?" I asked, pointing to the shoes.

"On the bottom. Over to one side. They were with all *that* stuff."

I opened my eyes wide. On Vanessa's messy bed were several hats, a book, and two small boxes. I must have missed them because I'd been so engrossed when I found the diary.

"What are these things?" I asked, rushing for them.

"Don't know," replied Vanessa. She was

gazing at herself in the mirror again. I had to admit that she looked uncannily like someone from another century. And I could almost *see* poetry forming in her head.

I shoved aside some of Vanessa's crumpled papers, sat on her bed, and opened the book. I was hoping for another year in the life of Sophie. But there were no words in the book at all, just pressed flowers. They were so crumbly and faded that they were hard to identify, but I thought that some of them might be pansies and others, violets.

I put the book down and gingerly opened one of the boxes. Inside was a pearl brooch (well, it might not have been made from real pearls) edged in gold.

"Ooh, Vanessa," I said. "Put this on. Isn't it pretty?"

Vanessa's eyes lit up.

"See? It goes right here on the collar of the blouse, at your throat."

I pinned the brooch on Vanessa and thought she would die of happiness. Then she tried on the hats while I opened the second box. It contained a different brooch, which I handed over to Vanessa.

"Who do you think all these things belonged to?" she asked dreamily, switching brooches.

45

"Sophie," I replied, just as dreamily.

"Who's she?"

"A girl who lived in the eighteen hundreds. She was born in eighteen eighty-two. Probably right in Stacey's house. I found her diary in the trunk."

"Gosh," was all Vanessa could say.

"Can you imagine living way back then?" I asked.

"And dressing like this every day?" added Vanessa.

"Maybe you didn't dress like that *every* day."

"Maybe you did if you were rich. Was Sophie rich?"

"I don't know. I haven't found that out yet."

"Stacey's house is nice, but it's not a mansion. I mean, it doesn't seem like a house for a *very* rich family," mused Vanessa.

"No, you're right," I agreed.

Vanessa turned back to the mirror, and I turned back to the diary. I opened it again and began to read the January 1st entry. But I closed the book. I decided I wanted to save it for good bedtime reading one night.

Instead, inspired by Sophie, I opened my own journal and began to write in it:

46

Today the most wonderful thing happened. I let the triplets break the locks on the trunk, and Vanessa and I found all sorts of marvelous things inside. Mostly we found antique clothes, but I also found a diary. It was kept by a girl just a year older than I, who lived more than a hundred years ago in Stacey's house.

I wonder what being twelve was like over a century ago. I can't wait to be twelve (better yet, thirteen) right now, but was it the same in 1894? Mom says that when I'm twelve I can wear any clothes I want. And she and Dad will start thinking about whether I can get contacts. What did Sophie's parents let her do? I will have to read to find out, but I am going to save the diary for a perfect night. That's the best way to read something you're looking forward to. Maybe it will be a dark and stormy night. Maybe — —

I stopped writing. I had just looked at the clock. Five-fifteen! I had to get to Claud's right away! I hid my journal (Vanessa never even noticed), ran downstairs, and hopped on my bike. Boy, did I have news for my friends!

CHAPTER 6

Today was my first tutoring session with Buddy. It was very difficult. I never realized how hard it is to be a teacher. I used to want to be one myself, but I'm glad I've decided to be a writer instead. I'm not going to give up on Buddy, though. I am going to make him into a reader. If I don't, he will miss out on too many things.

I tried to be optimistic in my journal, but I was feeling a little discouraged. I knew it wouldn't be my *fault* if I didn't turn Buddy into a reader, but I like good challenges and I *don't* like failing at them. Besides, I like Buddy, too, and I certainly didn't want to fail *him*.

My first session with Buddy fell on an afternoon when Mrs. Barrett had to work, but she was taking his reading problem quite seriously (even if she couldn't spend extra quality time with him), and had arranged for Jessi to babysit Suzi and Marnie, so that Buddy could have me to himself.

Jessi and I talked about the afternoon's arrangements on the playground at school that day.

"I think it's good that I get there first," said Jessi. "I'm supposed to arrive at three-thirty, right after school."

"And I don't arrive until four," I said. "Yeah, that is good. It'll be clear that you're the baby-sitter and I'm the tutor."

"You should probably work in Buddy's room at his desk with the door closed."

"Right," I agreed. "That'll be like school. Maybe Buddy needs help with things like concentrating and sitting still. A quiet room with a desk should be good."

Our plans were made. I was sure that tu-toring would be a snap. Sometimes I play spelling and writing games with Claire. She's always an eager student. So promptly at four that afternoon I rang the Barretts' bell, feeling excited. Inside, I could hear Jessi call, "Buddy, there's Mallory. That's for you. Can you answer the door, please?"

I was standing on the Barretts' steps, all smiles, ready to introduce Buddy to the wonderful world of reading.

But the door was opened by a boy with a scowl so big that my smile faded immediately. I tried to appear bright and perky, though.

"Hiya, Buddy," I said. "Are you ready to get to work?"

"No," he replied sullenly. "I just got home from school. I don't want to do more work."

But he let me in anyway.

I walked inside, called hello to Jessi and the girls, whom I could see in the kitchen, and led Buddy upstairs and into his room.

We closed the door.

"Now," I began, "first of all, we're going to sit at your desk, just like in school."

"You don't sit at my desk in school," said Buddy.

"Well, *you* do," I replied, "and I'm going to pull up your other chair and sit next to you. You can pretend I'm your teacher. Who's your teacher?"

"Mr. Moser. I hate him."

"Oh. Well, I guess I don't look much like him anyway. I'll just be Mallory then."

Buddy shrugged his shoulders as if to say, "Whatever. I don't care."

"Okay," I went on. "Your mom said your teacher sent home a box of flash cards. Let's start with those."

Buddy groaned. "I *hate* flash cards. Almost as much as I hate Mr. Moser."

"Well, let's try them anyway. Where are they?"

Buddy slapped his hand to his forehead. "Darn!" he cried. "I forgot and left them downstairs." He flew out of the room and took a long time coming back. But at last he returned with the flash cards.

"Here they are," he said grimly.

I opened the box.

"Oh, wait!" cried Buddy. "I forgot something else, too. I — I need a drink of water."

I let Buddy leave to get some water. He must be a camel. He was gone for an awfully long time.

When he returned, I resolutely closed the door to his room, cleared his desk of toys, sat him in the chair, and pulled the other chair up next to him.

I opened the box of flash cards. As I did so, I got an idea. I remembered the movie *Mary Poppins*, and how Jane and Michael's wonderful, magical nanny would make fun games out of boring things.

"Buddy," I said, "as we go through these flash cards, we'll put the words you know right away in one pile, and the hard words in another pile. For all the words you know — or learn today — I'll give you a minute of free time at the end of the afternoon, okay?"

Buddy looked mildy interested. "Okay," he agreed.

The cards in the box were all mixed up. On some were easy, short words. On others were hard, longer words.

I held up the first card.

"Easy," said Buddy. " 'At.' "

"Good. One minute of free time." I laid the card on the table and held up the second one.

Buddy stared at it. " 'Check'?" he guessed.

"Almost. The word is 'chicken.' " I laid it next to the first card.

"Do I lose my minute?" asked Buddy, dismayed.

"No, you just don't get a second one yet. That's all."

"Oh." Buddy still looked disappointed.

"Try this one," I said, showing him the next card.

"Ball," said Buddy. "Simple."

"Good. Now you have two free minutes."

We worked our way through about half the deck of cards. Buddy began to slump in his chair. He sat with one hand under his chin, as if his head might drop off if he didn't support it.

"Mallory," he whined, "I hate these cards. They're stupid. Sometimes I don't know a word all by itself, but if I see it in a book with a lot of other words around it, then I can figure it out." (Well, that made sense.) "Besides, look at the piles. There's a huge one of words I didn't get right away. The other pile is short. How many free minutes did I earn?"

I counted the cards in the small pile. "Seven," I told him.

"Seven! That's nothing."

Buddy looked like he was going to cry, so

I put the cards back in their box. "I guess we've spent enough time on flash cards. Do you have any homework?"

Buddy nodded. He told me what it was.

"Then how about reading in your reading book and doing the homework pages in your workbook?"

Buddy let out a huge sigh. Then he slapped his hand to his forehead again. "Darn! I forgot my reading book. I left it downstairs, too. I'll have to go get it."

"While you're at it, get your workbook," I said slyly. I just knew Buddy would "forget" it otherwise, and have to make yet another trip downstairs.

Buddy left, took his time finding the books, but finally returned with them. He was scowling again.

I ignored the scowl. "What did you say your workbook pages are?" I asked him.

"Sixty-seven and sixty-eight."

"Okay. Open to page sixty-seven."

Buddy did so.

"Now read the instructions out loud."

"Mallory," said Buddy, "I am not Cinderella. You can't order me around."

"Buddy," I replied, "I'm not your wicked stepmother, but I *am* your tutor, and it would

54

help if you followed directions."

"Oh, brother. All right." Buddy stared at the page. Then he stared out the window for awhile. I let him.

When he didn't give any indication of going back to the workbook pages, I said. "You just used up two minutes of your free time."

"What?!" Buddy shot me a look that I'm sure he usually reserved for Mr. Moser.

"Please read the instructions."

"*O-kay*." Buddy paused. Then he began reading. " 'On the page . . . below . . . are — are puh-puh . . .' "

I think Buddy was waiting for me to tell him the word. "Sound it out," I said.

"Pars?"

"Almost."

"Oh, pairs. 'Pairs of . . . wuh-words. Some . . . words ruh-ruh . . .' "

The word was "rhyme." How would he ever sound that out? "I'll give you a clue," I told Buddy. " 'All' and 'tall' are words that . . ."

"Rhyme!" cried Buddy, actually sounding pleased. He returned to the directions. " 'Some words rhyme and some words . . . donut.' I mean, 'don't. Cir-circle the rhyme words.' "

"The what?" I said.

" 'The . . . rhyming words.' "

"Good."

Buddy heaved another sigh and picked up his pencil as if it weighed a ton. He looked at the first pair of words, then at me, then at the words again. Maybe I was making him nervous. "I think I'll take a two-minute break," I said, "since you got one." I sat on Buddy's bed while he worked halfheartedly on the page. When I returned to the desk, Buddy had completed one column of words — and most of them were wrong. I made him go back, read the words to me, and do a lot of erasing. When the dreaded page was finally finished, Buddy said, "What time is it?"

"Five-fifteen," I replied.

"Five-fifteen? It's only five-fifteen?"

"Sorry," I said.

"I want to play with our video game."

"At five minutes of six you can do whatever you want."

"No fair," muttered Buddy, but he returned to his work.

What was I doing wrong? I wondered. I'd thought I would enjoy this. I'd thought Buddy would see what fun reading could be.

Nothing was going as I'd planned.

At long last I looked at my watch and said,

"Five of six, Buddy. You can stop working now."

"All *right!*" Buddy closed his reading book with a flourish. Then he took the books and the flash cards and stashed them under his bed — I guess so he wouldn't have to look at them.

As I walked back to my house I thought, There has got to be a better way.

CHAPTER 7

That night, Vanessa finished her homework early and went to the rec room to play with Margo and Claire.

I sat on my bed with a pencil and a pad of paper and tried to think of ways to make reading more interesting for Buddy. Why do I like reading? Because it's fun, I thought. Because it means something. Buddy's flash cards and workbook pages were not fun and they didn't mean much. The stories in his reader weren't much fun, either. But what could I do to change that? I didn't have any ideas, so I put the pad and pencil down. I picked up Sophie's diary instead. Suddenly, even though I hadn't finished my homework, and even though I didn't have any ideas for Buddy, I decided that tonight was the perfect night to read about Sophie's life in 1894.

I started at the very beginning. It was win-ter, of course, and Sophie seemed to have been invited to a lot of parties. Her family had known a lot of the other families in town. Maybe Sophie had been rich after all, despite the smallish size of her house. Or maybe in 1894, that *was* a big house. At the parties, Sophie and her friends played "parlour games," but Sophie didn't explain what they were. I would have to find out sometime.

Around the beginning of February, Sophie started mentioning a boy named Paul Hancock. Her diary entries got pretty mushy:

Oh, I love Paul so. How is it that he does not notice? I pine for him.

Blechh. I will never pine for a boy.
On February 11th, Sophie wrote:

Shall I send him a Valintine? He may laff at it. Worse yet, he may laff at me.... But I do love him so.

Sophie finally decided to send Paul a valentine card and, as it turned out, Paul was secretly pining for Sophie, so everything worked out okay.

I called Jessi to tell her what was happening

in Sophie's life. Then I went back to the diary. For a few weeks, all Sophie wrote about was school and Paul. Then Sophie's March 3rd diary entry said that her mother had just learned that she was going to have a baby:

At long last I shall have a sister or borther! I can barely wait. But the doctor has said that there may be complacatons. He said Mama shall have to stay in bed until the baby is born. Thinck of it! She must stay in her bed until Octuber. My, but Grandfather Hickman is mad. He said to my father, Jared, you are a scoundrel and a fool. You risk my daughter so that you might have a son. You will be the death of my daughter." I suppose he said that becuase Mama is frail and also his only child.

Whew! I had to call Jessi and read her that passage. Then I skimmed through spring and summer in the diary because I couldn't wait to find out what happened in October.

It was very sad.

Sophie's mother gave birth to a tiny baby boy, Edgar, but two days later she died. I couldn't believe it. I had to call Jessi again. And I knew I should finish my homework, but maybe if I woke up extra early the next morning, I could do it then.

I shouldn't have called Jessi so quickly, I soon realized, because Sophie's story just got more and more interesting . . . and mysterious. In fact, I had to call Jessi five more times — until Mrs. Ramsey said no more phone calls. Luckily, I'd told Jessi almost all of the story by then. This is what happened:

Three days after Sophie's mother was buried, a portrait of her disappeared from Sophie's grandfather's house. Mr. Hickman lived in a mansion across town. He was incredibly wealthy, and Sophie's family would come into a lot of money when he died. As it was, he gave them quite a bit of money while he was alive. Anyway, Grandfather Hickman accused Sophie's father, Jared, of stealing the portrait — and everyone in town believed him and shunned Sophie and her father and baby brother. Apparently Jared had sort of a shady past. In the first place, he came from a poor family, and Mr. Hickman called him a gold-digger. He said Jared only married his daughter for her money. But there was more to Jared than that. Before he got married, he had been arrested for stealing — twice. And he had a reputation for being violent. To be honest, he didn't sound like a very nice person. But Sophie wrote that he was her father, he had always been kind to her, and she loved him.

At any rate, when the painting disappeared, Grandfather Hickman wrote Sophie, Edgar, and Jared out of his will. And of course he stopped giving them money. At least he didn't make them move out of their house, which he also owned, but they didn't have much to live on and, because Hickman was a well-respected member of the community and Jared wasn't, hardly anyone would give Jared work. He took to selling firewood and doing little things like that.

You could tell that Sophie was furious. Her mother's portrait, she wrote, was not in *their* house, and anyway, she knew her father hadn't stolen it. She wanted his name cleared. It was unfair that he'd been accused just because of his bad reputation.

The last entry in Sophie's diary, on December 31st, read:

I vow to clear my fathers name. If I cannot do that, then I am certin that when he and I do eventually die, our spirits will remain in the house, uneasy, unable to rest. My only hope is that little Edgar shall grow up untainted.

As Claudia would say, "Oh, my lord. Oh, my *lord!*" And I had to wait until the next day to tell Jessi about this last diary entry? Impossible. I couldn't wait. I absolutely could not wait. . . . Could I? How do you keep from telling your best friend news like this?

Then — Just a second! I thought. Stacey's the one I should be telling. She was the one whose house Sophie and Jared would return to haunt.

Oh, my LORD!! Had Stacey and her mom bought a haunted house?

I looked at my watch. Almost ten o'clock. I couldn't call Stacey then. For one thing, it was too late at night to call a person and scare her with possible ghost stories. For another thing, it was bedtime. I could hear Vanessa and the triplets coming upstairs. At our house, the bedtime for anyone nine and older has recently been made ten o'clock. Now a Pike kid looks forward feverishly to his or her ninth birthday.

I waited patiently for a turn in the bathroom, washed my face, and brushed my teeth. When I returned to our room, Vanessa was already in bed. I quickly changed into my nightgown and hopped into my own bed.

"What were you doing up here all evening?" Vanessa wanted to know. "Homework?"

I shook my head.

"Thank goodness. I wouldn't go to middle school if I thought I was going to get so much homework."

I smiled. Then I decided to tell Vanessa the story of Sophie and Jared. Sometimes I tell her secrets, sometimes I don't. If I don't, it's usually because she's in one of her poetry-writing phases and wouldn't be paying attention anyway. Or else it's because I want to enjoy keeping the secret to myself.

But that night Vanessa wasn't lost in her thoughts — although she did look pretty sleepy — and no way could I keep the secret to myself.

"You will never guess what I was doing," I said to Vanessa.

"What?" (She never guesses.)

"Reading Sophie's diary. And you will never guess what I found out."

"What?"

"Guess, Vanessa, guess!" I cried. "You always just say 'What?'"

"You always tell me I'll never guess — so I never do."

I sighed. Then I told Vanessa not to take things so literally. And *then* I told her about Jared and Sophie and the missing painting. We were both in bed and the lights were out (after all, we were supposed to be asleep), and I have to admit I felt pretty spooked.

Vanessa must have felt that way, too. "Do you think the spirits of Jared and Sophie are roaming around Stacey's house right now?" she whispered.

"I don't know." I sat up in bed and looked out the window. It faced the backyard, but I couldn't see anything.

"When you think of it," I said, settling back into bed after a few moments, "an awful lot of people have moved in and out of that house. We've lived in ours for over twelve years — since before I was born. But I can think of at least six families or couples who have owned Stacey's house before she and her mom bought it. There must be a reason for that."

"Yeah . . ." said Vanessa softly.

"Plus, Stacey told me that her mother didn't have much money to spend on a house. That's how they wound up with Sophie's house. It's big and old . . . and it was cheap. Why would such a nice big old house be so cheap?"

"Don't know."

"Gosh, I wonder what really did happen to that portrait. But you know, if Jared *did* steal it, I can almost understand why. He might have wanted a reminder of his wife. But Sophie is *sure* her father *didn't* steal it. Besides, why steal something like that? You'd have to keep it hidden."

"Maybe just to have it close by," murmured Vanessa.

"Maybe. . . . I wonder if Sophie ever cleared her father's name. I mean, if he really was innocent. If she did, then we don't have to worry about ghosts over at Stacey's. But if she didn't, well, I certainly wouldn't want to live in a haunted house. And maybe all those people who lived there before Stacey moved in felt the same way. But they didn't tell the real estate agent why they were moving out because they were too embarrassed. I bet they made up other excuses — like an old house needs too many repairs. Or something like that. You know? . . . Vanessa? Vanessa?"

Silence. Vanessa was sound asleep.

I turned over and tried to fall asleep myself, but I was trembling with excitement. A haunted house. A century-old mystery to solve. It was all too much!

CHAPTER 8

Saturday

Well, thanks to you Mal, and your story about Sophie and Jared and the haunted house and missing portrait, I've got ghosts and attics on the brain. So today when I baby-sat for David Michael, Karen, Andrew, and Emily, I decided that exploring our attic would be a good project. It was raining, and we couldn't go outside (well, I guess we could have, but Emily is getting over a cold and another earache), and by the time Mom and Watson and everyone left, the kids were tired of their indoor toys. So I suggested that we go upstairs and see what's in our attic....

I hadn't been able to wait to tell the BSC members about my mystery, so I spread the word in school the next day, and at that afternoon's club meeting, we discussed things between job calls. Everyone was fascinated, of course, especially Stacey, but I didn't realize just how fascinated *Kristy* had been until I read her entry in the club notebook.

It was a rainy Saturday on the following weekend. It was also one of the weekends when Karen and Andrew, her little stepsister and stepbrother, were staying at their father's house. Kristy likes those weekends. It makes Watson's mansion feel fuller. More importantly, she loves being with Karen and Andrew.

Shortly after lunch, Kristy's mother and Watson took off for a meeting of the parents' council at the private school that Karen goes to and that Andrew and Emily will one day attend, and Nannie took off for bowling.

Kristy's grandmother is really neat. She doesn't seem like a grandmother at all. She has all these friends and hobbies and activities (being in a bowling league is one of her favorites), and she drives this rattly old car that she painted pink and calls the Pink Clinker.

After the adults had left, Kristy's big brothers went to a pep rally at Stoneybrook High — and Kristy's baby-sitting job began. She found herself facing four bored children.

David Michael, the oldest (he's seven, in case you forgot), whined, "I'm bo-*ored*." (David Michael can be a champion whiner.)

Karen, who's six and not a bad whiner herself, added, "I want to go out*si*-ide."

Andrew, four, just said, "Yeah."

And Emily asked hopefully, "Cookie?"

Kristy looked at her new little sister. Emily Michelle has short, jet-black hair and dark eyes that are so pleading they could make you say yes to anything. She's adorable. However, her speech is not great for a two-year-old. One reason is that the language she heard from birth until the time she boarded a plane to the United States was Vietnamese, and now she hears only English. Also, no one is sure what kind of care Emily got in the orphanage in Vietnam, but we're betting no one had much time to spend with *any* of the kids there. Emily's pediatrician in Stoneybrook calls her "language delayed," so the Brewers and Thomases have spent hours talking to Emily, reading to her, and trying to teach her words and phrases. When she makes the effort to ask for something in English, she usually gets it.

So when she asked for a cookie, Kristy said, "Sure!" Then, brightening, she added, "Why don't we all have a snack?"

"We just had lu-*unch*," whined David Michael.

Oh, boy, thought Kristy. The kids must really be bored if they're turning down food.

She got a cookie for Emily Michelle and tried to think of ways to entertain the children that afternoon. She knew she'd have to come up with something good. They'd already colored, watched *Sesame Street* and *Pee-wee's Playhouse*, played Candy Land and Chutes and Ladders, and built a fort with a moat around it out of blocks.

And then Kristy's great idea came to her. Her great ideas usually come out of the blue. I mean, she wasn't thinking about me or Sophie or the mystery right *then* — she was thinking about whining children — but she found herself saying excitedly, "Let's explore the attic!"

"The *attic?*" squeaked Andrew.

"The fourth floor?" cried David Michael.

"Where Boo-Boo won't go because of Ben Brewer's ghost?" added Karen.

"More cookie?" said Emily.

Kristy grabbed another cookie for Emily.

"The third floor," Karen began importantly, "and the attic above it are *both haunted*. You know that." She put her hands on her hips.

Karen believes in ghosts and witches. (I was beginning to understand why.) She believes that old Ben Brewer, Watson's great-grand-father, was haunted by a headless ghost, and then turned into a recluse. After he died, he became a ghost himself, and both he and the headless ghost haunt the third floor of the house (which no one uses), as well as the attic. Boo-Boo, Watson's old cat, refuses to go above the second floor, which Karen has told the other kids is a sure sign that the third floor is haunted. As she says, animals can sense those things.

Needless to say, the kids (except for Emily, who was too little) were afraid of the idea of exploring the attic, but Kristy could tell they were intrigued, too.

"Who knows what we'll find up there," said Kristy. Then, remembering the trunk and Sta-cey's attic, she added, "Old clothes to dress up in, maybe some old books. Even some old toys."

"Old skeletons," said Karen.

"Old ghosts," said Andrew.

"I doubt it," Kristy replied. "Come on. Let's just see what's there. If we find anything scary or hear any funny sounds, we'll come right back downstairs."

"*I'm* not afraid of ghosts," announced David Michael suddenly. "Especially headless ones. A headless ghost couldn't even see you."

"Ben Brewer isn't headless," Karen pointed out, but Kristy was already walking resolutely toward the stairs, and Karen and the others were following her.

Kristy carried Emily up the three flights of stairs because Emily is a slow, one-step-at-a-time stair-climber. Karen, Andrew, and David Michael huddled behind Kristy. When she paused at the top of the third flight and fumbled for the light switch, she wasn't sure what she'd find. Unlike Stacey's attic, which is small, Kristy's attic is the entire fourth floor of the house — room after room. But Kristy had never been past the head of the stairs, where she had dropped off stacks of magazines, or gone after Christmas tree ornaments. Watson keeps all the important things right there.

Now Kristy flicked on the light and walked boldly into the room and toward the first doorway she saw. The kids followed her like ducklings after their mother. They passed the Christmas decorations, boxes, and magazines, and found themselves in a room full of furniture, every piece covered with a white sheet.

"Aughh!" screeched Karen. "I think this is the furniture from Old Ben Brewer's room! Look, there's his bed . . . and his rocking chair . . . and his — "

"Aw, you don't know this stuff is Ben's," said David Michael, apparently on friendly terms with the dreaded ghost.

Andrew and Emily didn't say anything. Kristy had put Emily down, and she and Andrew were both gripping her hands.

Everyone wandered into the next room.

"Oh, cool!" Karen exclaimed. "Kristy was right. There *are* old toys up here!"

The room was a dusty mess, and it was dark, even with some light filtering through a dirty window, but it was the most interesting of the rooms so far. Karen had run to a brass doll's bed with two ancient-looking dolls nestled in it. Andrew found a set of tin soldiers. And Emily spotted a rocking horse, pulled Kristy over to it, and said, "Up?"

Of course, Kristy lifted her onto the horse right away and held her in place while Emily rocked happily. The kids had been playing in the quiet room for almost five minutes when, at the same moment, Emily said, "Down," and Kristy realized that David Michael wasn't there.

"David Michael?" she called.

Andrew and Karen looked up from their toys.

"Have you seen David Michael?" Kristy asked them.

They shook their heads.

"Oh, brother. You'd think he'd tell me if he was going back down — "

"Morbidda Destiny," interrupted Karen in a whisper.

"What?" said Kristy.

"The witch next door. I can see her house out the window. I bet she's a friend of Old Ben Brewer's and has powers in this attic and she and the ghosts have got David Michael — "

"BOO!!"

Everyone jumped a mile as David Michael burst out of an old wardrobe in a corner of the room. Emily began to cry.

"David Michael," said Kristy sternly, "you scared us to death."

"I'm sorry," he said immediately. "I didn't mean to make Emily cry. Honest. But wouldn't hide-and-seek be a good game to play up here?"

Everyone had to agree that it would, since they hadn't discovered all the hiding places already. So a game began. Kristy helped Emily dry her tears and then they worked together as a team.

The afternoon passed quickly. Kristy was looking for the zillionth hiding place that was big enough for both herself and Emily, when Karen, standing by a window, cried, "I see the Pink Clinker! I see the Pink Clinker! It's coming up the drive!"

"I think this is the end of hide-and-seek, you guys," said Kristy. "Let's go downstairs and see Nannie. She won't believe what we did today."

"Yeah," agreed Karen. "We stayed up in the attic for hours and didn't see a single sign of ghosts."

"Are you surprised?" asked Kristy, who confessed later that she'd been hoping for a *little* excitement, maybe a mystery like mine.

"I guess not," replied Karen. "Ghosts only come out at night anyway. This attic might be okay during the day, but I wouldn't want to come up here at night."

"Me neither," said Andrew and David Michael.

"Me neither," said Kristy.

She picked up Emily, and she and her brothers and sisters went downstairs to meet Nannie.

CHAPTER 9

Kristy was sitting in Claud's director's chair, her visor in place, a pencil stuck over one ear. She was wearing her usual jeans-and-turtle-neck outfit, and she was busy trying to get the meeting underway.

"Order! Come to order, please!" she was saying as she tapped a pencil on Claud's desk.

The rest of us were gathered and ready to go. Jessi and I were sitting on the floor, leafing through the club notebook. Jessi was wearing a long, heart-covered sweat shirt over her dance leotard and a pair of pink pants that (although you couldn't see this) I knew were held up at the waist with a drawstring. I was wearing boring old jeans, but a top that I liked a lot — a big white long-sleeved T-shirt that said I ♡ KIDS across the front.

In a row on Claud's bed were Mary Anne,

Stacey, and Claudia. Mary Anne, who can be pretty funky in her own shy way, was wearing a very cool short printed jumper over a striped shirt. You might think that those two things would clash, but they didn't. They looked great together. The jumper was white with a small red print, and the shirt was white with narrow, widely-spaced stripes. Claudia called the outfit "a fashion risk that worked." Claud herself was wearing jeans, a plain white blouse, a pink sweater, white socks, and loafers. She said she'd gone back to the fifties for the day. Stacey, on the other hand, was in a much more typical outfit — a short-sleeved blue-and-white jumpsuit with cuffed pants. Parts of it were striped, parts were solid. On her feet were high-topped sneakers laced only halfway up so that she could roll the tongue of the shoe down (*extremely* cool), plus she was wearing a lot of jewelry. I think Claud had made some of it for her.

Last but not least was Dawn, sitting backward in Claud's desk chair, resting her arms on the top rung of the back. Her outfit was fairly normal — pants and a baggy sweat shirt — but on her head was a small straw hat! I couldn't believe it. Talk about fashion risks.

Anyway, Kristy was calling us to order, and we were all straightening up and paying attention.

"Treasurer?" said Kristy to Stacey.

"Dues day!" Stacey cried (as if we could forget). "Pay up, you guys."

Grumbling and groaning, we reached into our pockets or purses and forked over the weekly dues. Stacey collected it, tossed it in the treasury, added up the new total (she can do this practically just by looking at the money), and announced what was in the manila envelope.

"Thirty-two dollars and forty-one cents. We're in good shape. Anybody need anything for the Kid-Kits?"

"Crayons," said Kristy.

"Can of Play-Doh," said Claudia.

"Stickers," I said.

Stacey handed each of us some money, reminding us twice to bring back the change. She looked as if parting with the money were painful.

Then the phone began to ring. After three job calls, things settled down. In fact, we reached a moment of silence.

"It must be twenty of six," said Jessi. "Silences are almost always at twenty of or twenty after the hour."

I stretched my head up to look at Claud's digital clock, the club's official timepiece. "Nope," I replied. "It's quarter of."

"Oh, well," Jessi said, and shrugged.

When a few more moments went by without another call, I said, "Um, Stacey? Have you noticed anything unusual at your house?"

"Unusual?" repeated Stacey. "Yeah. It got neat. Every last thing has been put away."

"That's not what I meant. I meant, have you noticed anything strange at night, in the dark, especially after you and your mom have gone to bed?"

"You mean like ghoulies and ghosties?" teased Claudia.

"Well . . . yes," I answered. "I'm serious, you guys. I'm dying to know if Sophie ever proved that her father was innocent. If there are no wandering spirits at Stacey's, it might mean that she did."

"It might also mean there are no such things as ghosts," spoke up Kristy.

"Come on, Stacey. *Have* you seen anything?" I asked again.

"We-ell, I have heard a few funny noises."

"Like what?" I asked excitedly.

"Oh, scratchings and blowings. Mom says I've forgotten what country nights are like. She says the noises are just squirrels or the wind. Stuff like that. One night I did see something white in my room. It was at the foot of my bed," (I heard Mary Anne draw her breath in sharply) "but I think it was just moonlight."

"Couldn't you tell for sure?" I asked. "Did it move or anything?"

Stacey shook her head. "Nope."

"Well, haven't you seen moonlight before?" I pressed.

"Only here in Stoneybrook. And at Camp Mohawk. In New York, it's impossible to tell moonlight from streetlights and lights from other buildings."

"Hmm," I said.

The phone rang then and we arranged a job for Mary Anne with the Perkins girls, who live in Kristy's old house.

When that was done, Kristy said, "You know, I've been thinking." (Isn't she always?) "We're going about this all wrong. We're solving the mystery backward. Instead of trying to find out whether Stacey's house is haunted, and then deciding if that means that Sophie and Jared's spirits are still hanging around —

which is pretty unlikely, all things considered — why don't we just try to solve the original mystery?"

"How can we do that?" I asked. "Everything happened over a hundred years ago."

"Oh, you never know what kind of information you can turn up once you start looking," replied Kristy. "For instance, we know that Sophie calls her grandfather 'Grandfather Hickman' and that he was rich and lived in a mansion across town from Stacey's house. You don't suppose Grandfather Hickman could have been *James* Hickman, do you?"

"Old Hickory?" squeaked Mary Anne.

"Oh, my lord!" exclaimed Claudia.

There's a legend in Stoneybrook about a recluse nicknamed Old Hickory, who was the meanest and stingiest, but also the wealthiest man in town, and who died decades ago, leaving his fortune to some long-lost nephew. In his will, he specifically said that he didn't want a big funeral or even a gravestone. But his nephew felt a little guilty, since he was inheriting so much money from someone he didn't even know, so he had a gravestone as big as a statue put up for his uncle in Stoneybrook cemetery. Now people say that the graveyard is haunted by the ghost of Old Hickory, who's angry about what his nephew did.

Mary Anne is particularly sensitive about this subject because some girls at school played a trick on her (well, on all of us, really) and made us go to Old Hickory's grave at midnight last Halloween. They had planned to scare us, but we ended up scaring them!

"Gosh, I wonder," said Dawn. "Grandfather Hickman . . . Old Hickory. And — and this is sort of a long shot, but you don't think Jared, Sophie's father, could be the Jared who's supposed to haunt the secret passage at my house . . . do you?"

"Oh, no," said Mary Anne quickly. "How could he be? Didn't the story go that he was the son of farmers who had to leave town in disgrace? Well, so far that much could be true. But then he disappeared. Wouldn't people have noticed if he turned up again and married the daughter of the richest man in town?"

"They're all just stories," Kristy pointed out. "And most of them are *ghost* stories, so right away we know we can't believe them entirely. What we have to do is find out which parts are accurate and see if anything connects."

"I should go back and check that old history book," said Dawn. "You know, *A History of Stoneybrooke*. I should read the part about Jared

Mullray again. I don't even remember when that story was supposed to have taken place. Hey, Mal, what's Sophie's last name? Is it Mullray?"

I paused. "I don't think Sophie ever mentioned her last name," I said finally. "At the beginning of the diary, she just wrote 'by Sophie.' I'm pretty sure the only last name she mentions is Hickman, but that wouldn't be *her* last name. I'll read through the diary again, though," I told Dawn.

"Well, one thing sort of fits," said Claud, our mystery-book fan. "If Sophie's grandfather really was Old Hickory, I think only he would be mean enough to hate Jared so much, no matter what Jared had done, and only he would cut two innocent kids out of his will just because he didn't like their father. After all, Sophie and Edgar didn't do anything to their grandfather."

"Hey!" exclaimed Jessi. "Maybe *Sophie* stole the painting. No one would suspect her. And that's how you usually solve mysteries, isn't it? You suspect the least suspicious person."

"Then we should suspect Edgar," I said. "Jess, Sophie wouldn't tell lies in her diary. That's not what diaries are for. If anything, she'd confess in it. Besides, she was too passionate. She couldn't lie so passionately."

"I think we can eliminate Sophie as a suspect," said Kristy. "But Claud does have a point about Old Hickory. He really might be Sophie's grandfather. And that's how you solve hundred-year-old mysteries. By connecting little pieces of information."

"I guess we still have some digging ahead of us," I said, "but I bet we can do it. I bet we can."

"Oh, I have goose bumps," said Mary Anne. "Even if this doesn't turn out to be another ghost story, it *is* pretty spooky. The missing portrait . . . the nasty grandfather . . . the dead mother."

"I *love* mysteries," said Claudia, hugging herself happily.

"Easy for you to say," spoke up Stacey. "*I'm* the one who might have angry ghosts roaming around my house at night." But I could tell she didn't really mean it. Stacey isn't a big believer in the supernatural or astrology or things like that. Even so, she looked just the teeniest bit nervous. The rest of us looked nervous, too. Claudia looked happily nervous, since she loves having a mystery to solve. Mary Anne looked worried and nervous, and everyone else, including me, looked intrigued and nervous.

All during our ghostly conversation we'd been stopping to take job calls. Now it was nearly six and the phone had stopped ringing. When Claud's digital clock read 6:00 on the nose, Kristy took off her visor and said loudly, "Meeting adjourned!" The BSC members left Claud's room, looking pretty thoughtful.

CHAPTER 10

It was another "Tutor Buddy" day. As you know, the first tutoring session had pretty much been a disaster. The second one hadn't been any better. But this time I was going to the Barretts' house armed with a few materials and a lot of ideas. I had finally put Sophie's diary down long enough to catch up on my homework and give some thought to Buddy's reading problems.

Ding-dong.

Buddy answered the doorbell, looking particularly unenthusiastic.

I ignored that. "Hiya," I said, sounding perky, as usual.

"Hi."

Buddy ushered me inside. Mrs. Barrett was home that afternoon and waved to me from the living room. When Buddy and I reached his bedroom, I saw Buddy's reader and workbook stacked neatly on his desk.

"Guess what?" I said. "We don't need those today." I pointed to his books.

"We don't?" replied Buddy. "Mom put them there so I wouldn't forget my homework."

"Well, we're not going to do your homework this afternoon. You can do it tonight. We'll look at your assignment before I go, to make sure you understand the directions. Now get this — we aren't even going to sit at your desk."

"Where are we going to sit?" asked Buddy, looking outdoors hopefully.

"On your bed. I've got something special for you."

"In that bag?"

"Yup. Come here and sit down." I patted a spot on Buddy's bed and turned on his reading lamp. When he had settled himself against a pillow, I sat next to him and handed him the bag.

"Is this for me?"

"Yup. Well, the things inside are on loan from Nicky and the triplets. We'll have to return them in a couple of days."

"Okay." Buddy looked intrigued.

Then he opened the bag and pulled out—

"Comic books? Archie comic books! What are they for?"

"They're for you to read," I told him. "I think they'll be more fun than your schoolbooks."

"Really?" cried Buddy. "I can read *these?*"

"Sure," I replied, but even as the word was coming out of my mouth, an awful thought was occurring to me. Maybe Mrs. Barrett didn't let her kids read comics. Some parents don't, and I can understand why. In our house we're allowed to read comics, but only as long as we read books, too. Mom and Dad said that was fair since they read some pretty junky magazines as well as good books. But not all parents feel that way.

Or maybe, I thought, Buddy's teacher doesn't let his students read comics. Or maybe Mrs. Barrett had said, "No comics until your grades improve, Buddy."

"You are allowed to read comics, aren't you?" I asked Buddy.

"We-ell, I don't know. My teacher said they're trash. But he didn't say we couldn't read them."

"What does your mother say?"

"About comic books? Nothing."

"Then we're going to read them," I said.

My reasoning was that Buddy didn't think reading was fun. He didn't enjoy it. If I could show him that reading *can* be fun, maybe (later) he would start reading things besides comics, like mysteries or animal stories. And when his reading improved, his schoolwork would become easier.

I fanned the comic books on the bed between Buddy and me. "Pick one," I told him.

Buddy considered the selection seriously. At last he chose a book. He opened it to the first page.

"I like comics!" he announced, sounding truly excited for the first time since I'd started tutoring him. "I like the pictures!"

"Try the words," I suggested.

Buddy drew in a deep breath — and began reading. He read haltingly at first. Then he began to sound more confident. When he stumbled over the words "ice-cream cone," I said, "Look at the picture. Does that give you a clue?"

"Oh!" he exclaimed. "Ice cream . . . I mean, ice-cream . . . cone?"

"You got it!"

"Hey!" Buddy sounded quite pleased with himself.

He read along. When he came to a word he

didn't know, he looked at the pictures and then sounded the word out. Buddy had been right. He could read more easily when he read words "together," instead of single words on flash cards. And he certainly read better when he liked what he was reading.

After Buddy had read two episodes in the comic book, I said, "Okay, we're going to stop now."

"Oh," groaned Buddy, "just when we were having fun."

"The next thing will be even more fun. I promise," I told him. "Do you have some notebook paper at your desk?"

Buddy nodded.

"Great. Go get it. And a couple of pencils with erasers, too, please."

Buddy did as I asked.

I took a piece of paper and, with a pencil, divided the paper into squares. Then I handed the paper back to Buddy. I put a book under it so that he could write on the paper.

"What's this for?" asked Buddy.

"Well," I began, "you've just read some comics. Now you're going to make your own. They can be Archie comics, or any comics. You could even invent new characters."

"I'm going to *make* a *comic strip?*"

"Sure," I replied. "I'll make one, too."

"I don't know, Mal," said Buddy. "I'm not very good at drawing."

"Just give it a try."

So Buddy sat and thought while I divided my own paper into squares. By the time I'd finished, he had begun working.

My comic was about a mouse, a squirrel, and a crow that lived in some woods and had adventures together. I was dying to peek at Buddy's paper and see what he was doing, but I didn't want to make him nervous.

Buddy worked and worked. He erased a lot. Every now and then he would glance at one of the Archie comics, probably to see how to make "thought bubbles" and things like that.

"Hey, Mal! This is fun!" said Buddy at one point.

I smiled at him. "I'm glad you think so. I'm having fun, too."

"Are you sure you're acting like a tutor?" asked Buddy.

"What do you mean?"

"I'm having too much fun. Reading work isn't supposed to be fun."

"But reading is. And reading and writing go hand in hand. Believe me."

Buddy shrugged. Then he returned to his

comic. After a few more moments of laborious effort he announced, "I'm finished!"

"Terrific. May I read it? You can read my comic."

"Okay," said Buddy uncertainly. "Are we going to read aloud or to ourselves?"

I thought for a moment. "We'll read each other's silently. Then we'll read our own aloud. We know how our own should sound."

Buddy grinned. "Okay."

So I read Buddy's comic. He had misspelled a lot of words, but he certainly had gotten the hang of the project. His comic was about three children (an older brother and his two younger sisters) with familiar-sounding names — Bubba, Sally, and Marie. The kids took an unexpected rocketship ride into outer space and then had to figure out how to get home again. The comic was full of things like this:

"Hey, Buddy, this is great," I said.

"Really?"

"Honest. I mean it. Let me hear you read it. I bet that will make it even better."

Buddy read his work with lots of expression and sound effects. When he was finished, he asked, "Can I show this to Mom?"

"Right now?"

"I'll only take a minute."

"Do you want to show her a *perfect* comic?" I asked.

"Yes," said Buddy, sounding a little confused.

"Well, then, I'll be honest with you. You spelled some words wrong. Would you like to fix them first?"

"Oh. . . . Yes."

"I'll give you a minute of free time for every word you misspelled that you can find and fix by yourself."

"Wow!" Buddy set to work and found nine of the seventeen words. "Nine free minutes!" he exclaimed.

"And I'll give you an extra free one for working so hard."

"Gosh." Buddy was looking at me adoringly. It was kind of the way I used to look at my fourth-grade teacher, Mr. Barnes. I had the world's biggest crush on Mr. Barnes. At the time, I thought I was in love with him. Was that how Buddy felt about me? I wasn't sure. If he did feel that way, maybe it wouldn't be such a bad thing. I've never worked as hard for any teacher as I did for Mr. Barnes. I got straight A's that year, something I'd never done before.

Anyway, Buddy showed his comic to his mother, but returned quickly to his room. "Now what are we going to do?" he asked.

"Now," I replied, "we are each going to choose one story in any comic book here, read half of it, and then make up our own ending to the story."

"Oh, boy!"

Buddy was in seventh heaven.

And I felt like a hero and a genius. Especially when Buddy decided to use his ten free minutes to begin his reading homework. (I think he did that because I was there to help him.) Whatever the reason, I felt as if I had made a breakthrough that day. I walked home feeling good right down to my toes.

CHAPTER 11

My life has certainly become more exciting lately. It's been awhile since I've written anything in this journal, so I better explain what is happening. My friends and I have not made much progress with Sophie's mystery. I reread her diary, trying to discover her last name, but she absolutely never mentioned it. Dawn was supposed to reread the part about the mystery at her house in the old Stoneybrook history book to see if there was any connection between Jared Mullray, the crazy farmer's son, and Sophie's father. But she hasn't been able to find the book. Dawn is the world's neatest person -- and her mother is the world's messiest, most scatterbrained person. So Dawn's room is a neat oasis in the messy desert of her house, and she knows the book is not in her room. That means it could be anyplace from on a shelf in the den to in the freezer in the kitchen. Or it might be over at Mary Anne's. Dawn and Mary Anne spend an awful lot of time together while their parents go out on dates. (Yes, dates! It's so exciting.) But Mary Anne is sure the book isn't at her house.

Anyway, since we've been making so little progress solving the mystery Kristy's way, I decided to go back to my own way -- trying to find out if Stacey's house has ghosts.

I decided that my friends and I should hold a séance....

"A séance! Are you kidding?" exclaimed Claudia.

"A séance?!" (That was Kristy.)

It was a Friday afternoon. Our BSC meeting was just about over. In the few minutes that were left, I had mentioned my idea to the other club members. As you can see, it was not going over too well. Although in all honesty, I have to admit that I thought most of my friends were *afraid* of holding a séance, and were covering up by acting appalled.

"Yes," I told them firmly. "A séance."

"Um, Mal?" spoke up Jessi. "What *is* a séance?"

Before I could answer, Kristy said. "It's when a person wearing a turban on her head goes into a trance and the voice of George Washington comes out of her mouth. Then she collapses on the table from the effort of it all."

"Kristy!" I exclaimed.

"Huh?" said Jessi.

"A séance," I said, "is when a group of committed people get together in the hope of contacting a spirit. They sit around a table holding hands, and one person — the channeler — calls for the spirit. If the spirit is around, it begins speaking through the channeler. Then the others can ask the spirit questions." I gave Kristy a look to let her know just what I thought of *her* explanation.

"Oh," said Jessi. "And you want us to try to contact Sophie so we can find out what happened with the portrait?"

"Right. Or Jared would do, I guess. We'll hold the séance at Stacey's house."

Stacey groaned.

"What if we can't contact Sophie or Jared?" asked Jessi.

I shrugged. "Then we'll be no worse off than we are right now."

"There aren't any such things as ghosts or spirits anyway," said Kristy for about the ninetieth time.

"You know what?" said Dawn, who had been sitting quietly on the bed. "A séance might be kind of interesting." (Dawn loves ghost stories as much as Claudia loves Nancy Drew mysteries.)

Mary Anne shivered. "Spooky, but interesting," she added.

"It could be funny," said Stacey, glancing at Kristy. I could tell that the two of them were trying not to laugh.

Mary Anne opened the club record book to the appointment pages. "We're all free tomorrow afternoon," she said. "Not one of us has a job, a class, or a lesson."

"Mary A-anne," said Kristy, who is almost as good a whiner as David Michael.

"Oh, come on. Maybe it'll be fun," said Stacey. "What harm can it do, anyway? We can have sort of a séance party. I'll buy some chips and stuff, the seven of us can get together, and who knows? We just might talk to Sophie or Jared."

"*Sta*-cey," said Kristy.

"*I* think it sounds like a great idea," said Claudia.

"Me, too," said Dawn, Mary Anne, Jessi, and I.

Everyone looked at Kristy.

"Oh, all right. I'll come," she said. "But only if I can be the channeler."

Kristy the channeler? This was my mystery and my idea. *I* wanted to be the channeler. But one problem with being eleven and having a lot of thirteen-year-old friends is that you have to give in to them pretty often, especially when someone like Kristy is putting her foot down.

"Okay," I said. "You can be the channeler."

We agreed to meet at Stacey's at four o'clock the next afternoon.

By 3:45 on Saturday, everyone except Kristy had arrived at Stacey's house. I guess my friends were a little more excited about the séance than they'd let on.

"Where do you hold a séance?" asked Dawn.

"We should hold ours in the attic," replied Stacey promptly. "That's where we found the trunk. And it seems like a good place for ghosts."

"A little *too* good," said Mary Anne. "I'm not going up into your attic to try to contact dead people. I've got goose bumps just thinking about it."

"I don't think that would work anyway," I spoke up. "I've seen lots of séances on TV, and everyone is always sitting around a table holding hands. You don't have a big table in your attic, do you, Stace?"

"Nope," she replied. "Not even room for one. If we *really* need to use a table, it'll have to be the kitchen table or the dining room table. Probably the dining room table. It's bigger. Seven people would be squished around the kitchen table."

We were just heading into the dining room when the doorbell rang.

"That must be Kristy!" cried Stacey.

The six of us dashed to the McGills' front door.

When we opened it, we gasped.

On the doorstep stood a gypsy.

Well, it was Kristy, but she looked like a gypsy. She'd put on false eyelashes and bright red lipstick, and on her cheeks were big blotches of rouge. Her clothes were amazing. She was wearing a baggy peasant blouse; a long, flowing skirt with gaudy flowers printed on it; and *tons* of jewelry — beads around her neck and bangles up each arm. On her head was a turban.

Kristy entered the front hall, her jewelry clanking as she walked.

"Oh, my *lord*," said Claud, her voice rising. "Where did you get all that stuff?"

"The makeup is Nannie's. The rest I found in our attic. Well, Karen did. She was looking for dress-up clothes, and boy, did she ever find them."

Stacey shook her head. Then she ushered the BSC members into her dining room. "Okay," she said. "Let's begin."

"Where's the food?" asked Kristy.

"Kristy!" I exclaimed. "The food is for afterward. A séance is serious. We can't be eating potato chips and trying to contact Sophie at the same time."

"Okay, okay," said Kristy. "And by the way, my name is Madame Kristin."

"Yes, Madame Kristin," said Claudia, bowing.

"All right, everybody. Gather around the

table. We have to hold hands, close our eyes, and concentrate really hard," I said.

"On what?" asked Claudia.

"On Sophie! What else? We have to think, *Sophie, Sophie, join us in our world.* And Kristy, I mean, Madame Kristin, you have to say that out loud — and do whatever else you do to contact spirits."

"What else is that?"

"You're the channeler. I thought you knew."

"*You're* the séance expert. I thought *you* knew."

"I'm not a séance *expert.* I've just seen some séances on TV."

"Hey, hey, you guys," said Mary Anne, who likes to avoid a fight if at all possible. "Kristy, why don't you just improvise?"

"Okay," agreed Kristy, rattling her bracelets. "And it's *Madame* Kristin."

The seven of us sat down at the dining room table. But right away, I jumped up again.

"What's wrong?" asked Jessi.

"Atmosphere," I replied. "We forgot atmosphere. We can't hold a séance with sunshine pouring through the windows."

I got up and pulled the curtains across the dining room windows. Then I closed the doors to the dining room. We were in semidarkness.

"Stacey? Do you have any candles around?" I asked.

"Sure." Stacey found three fat, short candles in holders. She set them in the middle of the table and lit them with a long fireplace match. Candlelight danced on the walls.

"Ooh, spooky," said Jessi.

"Do we have enough atmosphere now?" asked Madame Kristin.

"I think so," I replied.

Stacey and I returned to our seats.

"Now, everybody hold hands," I instructed. "Think about Sophie or Jared. Call them to our world — silently. Except for you, Madame Kristin. You speak out loud."

"I know, I know," she said.

I was sitting between Jessi and Mary Anne. Jessi's hand was shaking. Mary Anne's was clammy. I hoped they would calm down.

Sophie, I said to myself, if you can hear my thoughts, come meet us in our world, in the world of the living. We need to talk to you.

"Sophie," Kristy was saying in an eerie voice, "come to me. Speak through me. You — you will not be harmed. We just want to ask you some ques — " Suddenly, Kristy's voice changed. It rose and became all wavery.

"I . . . am . . . heeeere," she wailed. "I am Sophie and I am heeeere."

I gasped. Then I held my breath. I didn't want to frighten Sophie away.

"Speeeeak to meeee," said Sophie.

"Sophie," I said, "this is Mallory Pike."

"I knoooow."

"You do?"

"Yes. I know everythiiiing."

"Did — did you find the painting and clear your father's name?"

"Yeeees."

"Where was the painting?" asked Dawn.

"It had never disappeared. It was hanging where it always huuuung. But Grandfather Hickmaaaan, God rest his soooooul, lost his glasses and just thought it had disap-peeeeared."

"Really?" I asked.

Madame Kristin burst out laughing. "Of course not, you goon," she said in her regular Kristy voice. "I can't get Sophie to speak through me. Are you crazy? Now let's party. I'm starved!"

So that was the end of our séance. I wasn't too mad. I think I'd known all along that we wouldn't really be able to contact Sophie. Besides, I was hungry, too!

106

CHAPTER 12

Tuesday

Sat for Charlotte Johanssen today. I am so happy to be sitting for her again. I didn't realize how much I missed her when I was in New York. Charlotte is just the greatest little girl. If I ever get married and have a kid, I hope I have a daughter just like Charlotte. For one thing, she is smart. Well, we all know she skipped a grade. But she's not just schoolbook-smart, she's thoughtful-smart, too. I know this probably doesn't make much sense, so I better try to explain. What happened was that I told Charlotte about our mystery with Sophie....

Stacey has said that when she left New York, she didn't just leave her dad, her apartment, and one of her best friends behind. She also left behind two of her favorite baby-sitting charges — Henry and Grace Walker. So she was especially glad that Charlotte was still in Stoneybrook. And as soon as she returned, she became one of Charlotte's most frequent sitters again. Everyone — Stacey, Charlotte, Dr. and Mr. Johanssen — were pleased with the turn of events.

On that Tuesday, Stacey arrived at Charlotte's house with her Kid-Kit. Charlotte has always been a big fan of the Kid-Kits, so Stacey usually brings hers when she sits at the Johanssens'.

Charlotte answered the doorbell, excited as always to see Stacey.

"Hi!" she said. "Come on in!"

Charlotte used to be this shy, withdrawn little girl, but Stacey helped to pull her out of her shell. It wasn't easy, but she did it. Then, when Jessi and her family moved to Stoneybrook, Jessi helped Charlotte and her younger sister, Becca, to become friends.

Now Charlotte, who is an only child, is bouncy and happy and hardly minds at all when her mother, a doctor, goes off to work at the hospital.

"Hi, Stacey!" Dr. Johanssen called as Stacey entered the house.

"Hi!" Stacey replied. She and Dr. Johanssen get along really well.

"How are you feeling these days?"

"Great. I stick to my diet and give myself the shots and I haven't been sick in ages."

"That's wonderful," Dr. Johanssen replied warmly. Then she said, "Well, I better get going. You know where the emergency numbers are. Mr. Johanssen will be home before six o'clock. So just go ahead and have fun. Oh, and if Becca wants to come over, that's fine."

"Okay," Stacey said. But as it turned out, Charlotte never even thought about Becca. And she didn't open the Kid-Kit for quite some time.

That was because as soon as Dr. Johanssen left, Stacey said, "Guess what. My friends and I are trying to solve a mystery."

"Really?" asked Charlotte, wide-eyed.

Stacey could tell she loved the idea of a real mystery, like the ones she reads about in books. Charlotte is an extremely good reader. She reads anything from The Bobbsey Twins to books by Roald Dahl to books for older kids, like *A Tree Grows in Brooklyn*.

"Yup," Stacey said. "See, right after we moved in, Claudia and Mallory were helping me put some stuff in our attic, and while we were up there, we found an old trunk, and in the trunk, Mallory found a diary that was written in eighteen ninety-four by Sophie, a twelve-year-old girl. And she lived in *my house* then. Or at least, we think she did. Anyway, her mother died, and right away this portrait of her mother disappeared."

Stacey told Charlotte the whole story.

"Wow," said Charlotte when Stacey had finished. "And you really think Sophie's grandfather was Old Hickory?"

"We really do."

Stacey and Charlotte were sitting on the floor of the living room with the unopened Kid-Kit between them. This is one of their favorite places in which to spend time. The Johanssens never mind, as long as Stacey and Charlotte don't make a mess.

"You know what?" said Charlotte after thinking for a moment.

"What?" asked Stacey.

"I don't believe there's any mystery that can't be solved."

110

"You don't? How come?"

"Because somebody always knows something. Somebody took the painting or somebody hid it, and maybe someone saw what happened. And if no one saw, then at least the thief knows what he did. And chances are, he'll make a mistake sometime and his secret will be out."

"But Charlotte, this happened more than a *century* ago," Stacey pointed out.

"Yeah, but you never know. There is — or was — a culprit somewhere. And he probably slipped up, or someone saw him. I bet you can solve this mystery. It's pretty hard to commit the perfect crime."

Stacey giggled. "Have you been watching *Crime Court* on TV again?"

"Yes," admitted Charlotte, beginning to laugh, too.

"Well, I still don't know," said Stacey. "About solving the mystery, I mean. It's a pretty old one."

"You guys just don't know the whole story yet, that's all," Charlotte told her. "I'll show you something. Wait right here, okay?"

"Okay," said Stacey.

Charlotte ran upstairs, probably to her room, and returned with a dog-eared book.

"This used to be my mom's," Char told Stacey. "It was her book when she was a little girl and then she gave it to me. It's really too easy for me now, but I like it anyway. It's called *Katie and the Sad Noise*, and it's by Ruth Stiles Gannett. Can I read it to you?"

"*May* I read it to you," Stacey corrected her.

"Okay, may I read it to you?"

"Of course." Stacey patted the floor next to her. "Sit here."

Charlotte shook her head. "I have to read to you from across the room. I don't want you to see the pictures yet."

"Oh. All right," replied Stacey, mystified.

Charlotte settled herself in an armchair and held the book flat in her lap so that Stacey couldn't even see the cover. Then she began to read. The story was about a little girl named Katie who had been hearing a sad noise in the night. During the day she would go out and look for the noise, but she couldn't find anything. Her parents were worried about her. They thought she was imagining things. But soon other people started to hear the sad noise — even Katie's mother. So the whole town went on a search, and finally they found a mother dog with four puppies in the woods, and the mother dog's foot was caught in a trap. The sad noise was the dog crying to be released from the trap. The story had a happy ending because the dog and her puppies were rescued.

"That's a nice story, Char," Stacey began, "but I don't see — "

"Wait. Now let me show you the pictures," Charlotte interrupted. She scrambled out of the chair and over to Stacey on the floor.

"Hey!" said Stacey, flipping through the book. "This is a Christmas story! Look, Katie's parents are decorating the tree in this picture, and on this page there are Christmas decorations up at Katie's school."

"Right," said Charlotte. "Only you'd hardly know this is a Christmas story if you didn't see the pictures. Christmas is only mentioned twice, and you don't know if it's right around the corner, or a whole month off. Not unless you see the pictures."

"But Charlotte, I *still* don't see what this book has to do with Sophie and Old Hickory and our mystery. What are you trying to tell me?"

"Only," replied Charlotte, "that things aren't always what they seem to be. Sometimes you have to look past what's right in front of your nose."

Well, Stacey puzzled over that for the rest of the afternoon. She puzzled over it while Charlotte puzzled over our mystery. She puzzled over it while she read two chapters of *The BFG*, by Roald Dahl, to Charlotte. She puzzled over it while Charlotte beat her at Memory and she beat Charlotte at dominoes. She puzzled over it while Charlotte began her homework. And she puzzled over it while Mr. Johanssen paid her and she rode her bike home.

She called me right away.

"Mal?" she said. "It's me, Stace. I just got back from sitting for Charlotte and she said something pretty interesting."

"What?" I asked. I was talking on the phone in our upstairs hallway, where there is absolutely no privacy.

"She said, 'Things aren't always what they seem to be.' " Stacey explained about *Katie and the Sad Noise*. "I wonder what this has to do with our mystery."

"I'm not sure," I replied, "but I'll think about it. I like what she said about someone knowing something, too. About there always being a culprit. Maybe Kristy's right after all. Maybe the pieces to the mystery are all here to be found — if we just look past our noses."

"Maybe," said Stacey uncertainly. "I hope so."

"I know so," I replied, suddenly optimistic.

CHAPTER 13

"So, Buddy, what did you think?" I asked him.

I was tutoring Buddy again and had come over with some more special materials. I think Buddy had been hoping for comics. Instead, I had brought over a collection of Encyclopedia Brown mysteries. The fun thing about Encyclopedia Brown is that you — the reader — can *really* solve the mysteries yourself. If you pay close enough attention to each short story you can find the clue and solve the mystery, instead of just reading about how Encyclopedia Brown, boy detective, solves it.

So I read one story out loud to Buddy — and he solved the mystery right away!

"That is ter*rif*ic, Buddy!" I exclaimed. "I bet I couldn't do that."

"Bet you could."

"Could not."

116

"Could. Here. Let me read a mystery to you. Then you'll see." Buddy took the book out of my hands and read an entire mystery with only a few mistakes. His reading was *so* much better. When he finished, I knew the solution right away — but I pretended I couldn't figure it out.

"Gosh, I don't know, Buddy — " I began.

"Come on, *think*," said Buddy, probably the way Mr. Moser sometimes spoke to him. "What did the bully say to Encyclopedia right near the end — "

"Oh, *I* know!" I cried. "I've got it!" I told Buddy the solution.

"That's it! Now let's do another. This time you read a story to me again."

Buddy and I were sitting cross-legged on his bed, facing each other.

I took the book back from him, but instead of selecting another mystery, I said, "You know, my friends and I are in the middle of a *real* mystery."

"No kidding," said Buddy.

"Yup." I told him about the trunk and the diary. The more I talked, the wider Buddy's eyes grew.

When I had finished the story — including the part about the séance — Buddy was so excited he was wriggling around on the bed. "Can I see the diary? Can I, Mallory? *Please?* I want to read about Sophie's mystery. Maybe I could solve that one, too. Maybe I could be a detective like Encyclopedia Brown!"

At first I thought, Buddy is just looking for an excuse to get out of his tutoring session. But then I decided that if he *really* wanted to look at the diary, that would be just as good a reading experience as any other. Probably better, since Buddy was so interested in solving the mystery.

"Okay," I said. "I don't see why we can't go to my house. You can look at the diary there. But I better warn you. It isn't easy to read. Even *I* had trouble with it. The words aren't really long or anything but, well, can you read cursive yet, Buddy?"

"Yup," he replied proudly.

"All right then. Let's go."

Buddy and I dashed downstairs. While Buddy put his jacket on, I explained to Mary Anne what we were doing. (Mary Anne was sitting for Suzi and Marnie that afternoon.)

"Good luck!" Mary Anne called after us as we ran out the Barretts' front door.

Buddy was so excited that he kept right on

running, all the way to my house. When I opened our door for him, he ran up to Vanessa's and my room.

Vanessa was surprised, to say the least, to see Buddy appear breathlessly before her.

"What's going on?" she asked. She was in a poetry-writing phase, surrounded by papers. I hoped we hadn't broken her train of thought. "This isn't Nicky's room, Buddy," she said. "And he isn't home anyway."

"I'm not here to see Nicky," replied Buddy, undaunted.

"He's here to see the diary and the trunk," I said.

"Hmphh." Vanessa huffed out of our room with an armload of papers.

"Is that the trunk?" asked Buddy excitedly, pointing to it.

"It sure is," I answered. I was proud of the trunk. I had cleaned it and polished it and even tried to fix the broken locks. It looked more beautiful than ever.

"Where's the diary?"

"Right here." I retrieved the diary from my nightstand and Buddy and I sat next to each other on my bed.

Buddy opened the diary carefully. He

flipped to January 1st and just stared at the page. "Gosh," he said after a moment, "this *is* hard to read."

"I know. The ink is faded and Sophie had funny handwriting."

"She couldn't spell, either," said Buddy, and we both laughed.

"Good for you," I said. "What did you find wrong?"

"This word. *Happy.* She only put one 'p' in it. You would have to pronounce that 'hay-py.' "

"You're absolutely right." I wanted to hug Buddy. If only Mr. Moser could see him now. He would probably send a nice note home to Mrs. Barrett.

Buddy struggled along with the diary for about ten minutes, sometimes reading to me, sometimes to himself. When he reached the middle of January, he said, "This is really boring. Where's the mystery?"

"You have to skip way ahead to when Sophie's little brother was born," I told him. I flipped through the diary. "There. Start reading there."

Buddy did. To himself. He read for so long that *I* got bored and began to read a new horse story I'd borrowed from the library. It was after five o'clock when Buddy suddenly closed the diary.

I closed my book, too, and glanced over at him.

"I couldn't find the clue," said Buddy, looking disappointed.

"Well, don't feel too bad," I told him. "No one else has found any clues, either. This isn't Encyclopedia Brown, you know."

"Maybe the clue's not in the diary," said Buddy, as if he hadn't heard me. "Maybe it's somewhere else, like in the trunk. Could I look in the trunk, Mal?"

"Sure," I replied. "Just be really careful. Some of the clothes in there are so old they're falling apart."

"Okay."

Buddy opened the trunk and began feeling around. He dug deeper and deeper through the clothes until —

"Uh-oh," he said.

"What-oh?" I asked.

"Mallory, my hand is stuck."

"Stuck? How could it be stuck?"

"It just *is*."

I got up and felt around in the trunk. I followed Buddy's arm down, down until . . .

"It *is* stuck!" I exclaimed.

121

"Told you so."

"It's in a sort of pocket, I think." I moved aside some clothes and tugged on Buddy's arm. At last his hand came loose. It *had* been stuck in a pocket (a very well-hidden one), and it was now clutching a packet of papers.

"Look what was in there!" said Buddy.

We spread the papers out on my bed. Like the pages of the diary, they were old and yellowed, only some of these were actually crumbling, so we had to be extremely careful.

Buddy looked at the page numbered "one." He bent over so he could read it without touching it. "James Hickman," he said. "My Confession."

Buddy and I looked at each other, our mouths open. Then Buddy began to read out loud, but I was too excited to listen to his slow, careful pronunciation. For just a while, I couldn't be his tutor. I skimmed ahead silently.

It turned out that Grandfather Hickman really *was* James Hickman — so Kristy had been right. He was also Old Hickory, of course. And you will never guess what he did. People might have thought Jared was a mean guy, but he wasn't half as terrible as Old Hickory. Although I have to admit that if you can believe Old Hickory's confession, he didn't *set out* to do something terrible. He just *allowed* something terrible to happen.

Old Hickory wrote that after his daughter died, he was distraught and couldn't even bear to look at her portrait. He didn't want to get rid of it, though, so he hired someone he called an "itinerant painter" to paint *over* the portrait of Sophie's mother. (I found out later that an itinerant painter was an amateur artist who made his living going from town to town painting portraits and other pictures for people who wanted "art" in their homes.) Then Old Hickory changed the frame around the painting and moved the new painting into another room in his house. That way his daughter was with him — and yet she wasn't.

Okay, that much I could understand. But then Old Hickory's friends (I guess he hadn't become a recluse yet) began asking where the portrait was. Old Hickory was embarrassed about what he'd done, so he lied and said the painting had disappeared, had probably been stolen. Immediately, the townspeople suspected Jared. They knew how Old Hickory felt about him — that Jared was a good-for-nothing who had married Sophie's mother for her money and then insisted that she have another child when she was really too weak for it. And the terrible thing that James Hickman had done was to *let the people believe they were right*. He never admitted to having the portrait painted over — not until he was old and ready to die and bursting with his secret. Then he wrote out his confession, knowing that someday someone would find it and learn the truth.

"Whoa," said Buddy when he'd finally finished reading the confession and I had helped him understand the hard parts.

"I know," I said. "Double whoa. What a find you made, Buddy! I'm glad you got your hand stuck. Maybe you *will* become a detective one day."

"Maybe," said Buddy. "You know, detectives ask a lot of questions, and I have one right now."

"What is it?"

"How did this trunk with Old Hickory's confession in it turn up in the attic of Sophie's house — with Sophie's diary and clothes in it?"

I frowned. "Good question," I said. "Maybe when Old Hickory's nephew inherited the mansion, he moved some things he didn't want over to Sophie's house. Old Hickory

owned that house, too. The trunk was probably half empty, and the nephew just dumped
some stuff into it."

"Hey!" cried Buddy. "If the nephew moved
the trunk to Sophie's house, he might have
moved some other things over there, like, say,
an old *painting!*"

"Whoa," I said again.

CHAPTER 14

"**B**uddy, you're a genius!" I exclaimed.

Buddy blushed. "Maybe, maybe not. I'm just guessing."

"But your guess is a good one. Come on, let's call Stacey and see if she's home. It's almost five-thirty. We still have half an hour before I have to get you back to Mary Anne. We have just enough time to take a look around Stacey's attic."

"Oh, boy!" cried Buddy.

I was on the hall phone dialing Stacey in about two seconds.

"Stace! Stace!" I said. (I'd been so afraid she wouldn't be home.)

"Mal? Is that you? Is everything all right?"

"Yeah, it's me, and everything is better than all right. You will not believe what Buddy found today!"

I told her how Buddy and I had come over

to my house, and Buddy had gotten his hand stuck and found the confession. Stacey sounded somewhat confused — until I told her our theory about Old Hickory's things winding up in her attic. Then she got the point immediately.

"The painting!" she shrieked. "Oh, wow! Come over right now! Both you and Buddy. We'll make a thorough search. It shouldn't take too long, since the attic's so small and we've cleared some things out."

"You haven't cleared out any paintings, have you?" I asked, horrified.

"Nope. So come over now."

Buddy and I probably broke a record getting from our phone to Stacey's front door. I barely took the time to yell to Mom that Buddy and I were going to the McGills'. Then, when Stacey let us in, the three of us probably broke another record getting to her attic. If nothing else, we broke a noise record. I know because Mrs. McGill yelled from downstairs, "What on earth is going on? I have never heard so much noise!"

But we ignored her and burst into the attic as if we were cops busting a pair of bank robbers or something.

As soon as we were in the attic, though, we

came to a screeching halt. We weren't sure what to do first.

"Let's each explore a different area of the attic," I finally suggested. "Buddy, you take that end under the window. It's pretty crowded. Stacey, you take that side, and I'll take the other side."

So we split up. Now that we were looking for something in particular, we came across all sorts of unusual things. Stacey found a helmet that Buddy said was a soldier's helmet from the First World War. (How did he know that?) I found a dusty music box that played "The Waltz of the Flowers," and Buddy found an ancient set of magic tricks. (Stacey said he could have them.) And *then* Buddy made what we thought was the find of the day.

"Oh!" he cried. "Wow! Back here! Behind these filing cabinets. There's a whole *stack* of paintings. They're leaning against the wall!"

Stacey and I rushed over. We tried to examine the paintings, but the attic was too dark in that corner. Stacey had to leave to get a flashlight. When she returned, we shined it on all the paintings, one by one.

"How would we know if something's been painted over?" Buddy wondered.

"Or what kinds of things an 'itinerant

painter' would paint?" added Stacey.

We were getting ready to give up when I said, "Wait, I haven't finished exploring my area yet." I returned to it with the flashlight, leaving Buddy and Stacey examining the magic tricks.

"Hey, here's another painting!" I called, finding one propped against an old bureau.

"What's it of?" asked Buddy.

"Ships," I replied.

"Let's give up," said Stacey.

"Yeah," agreed Buddy. "I'm hungry. I want to go home for din — "

Buddy never got to finish his sentence. That's because I suddenly screamed, "Oh, I don't believe it!"

"What?" said Stacey.

"I think this *is* the portrait of Sophie's mother!"

"Oh, right," scoffed Buddy. "Ships."

"Ships sailing over a finger with a ring on it?" I said triumphantly.

Buddy and Stacey nearly trampled each other trying to reach me.

"Where? Where?" cried Stacey.

I shined the flashlight on the lower right-hand corner of the painting. "See?" I said. "The paint has chipped away. There's another painting under the ships. What do you bet it's the portrait?"

"I'd bet a lot of money," said Stacey.

"Me, too," added Buddy contritely.

"What should we do now?" I asked.

"Let's carry it downstairs and show it to my mom," said Stacey. "She's poring over the want ads in the paper. I'm sure she'd be glad to take a break."

So Stacey and I carried the painting downstairs, and Buddy followed us with the box of magic tricks. Needless to say, Mrs. McGill was a little surprised when Stacey and I lugged the painting (which was pretty ugly, by the way) into the kitchen and leaned it against the refrigerator. She gave the three of us a look that plainly said, "What is going *on?*"

So then I had to tell her the entire Sophie story, which was longer since we'd found the confession and the painting. Truthfully, I was getting a little bored telling the story.

But Mrs. McGill didn't look bored hearing it. In fact, she looked fascinated. Her eyes grew even wider than Buddy's had grown when I'd told him the story.

"How will we know if this is really the portrait?" asked Stacey.

"Let's get some turpentine!" suggested Buddy.

"No," said Mrs. McGill quickly. "We wouldn't know what we were doing. We'd wipe away *all* the paint and lose the portrait, too. I think we should take the painting to a professional art restorer. There's probably one in Stamford."

"Would you really do that?" I exclaimed.

"Of course," Stacey's mother replied. "I'd like to see an end to this mystery, too. After all, I don't want any ghosts around here, either."

"Oh, *Mom*," said Stacey, but I could tell she was pleased with what her mother was going to do.

At that moment, I looked at my watch and saw that it was 6:05.

"Oh, my gosh, Buddy!" I cried. "We're late. I was supposed to have you home five minutes ago." And at that moment, the phone rang. It was my mother saying that Mrs. Barrett had said that Mary Anne had said that Buddy and I were going to go to my house and where were we?

I ran Buddy home. By the time we got there, Mary Anne had left, and Mrs. Barrett was looking pretty worried. So I had to tell Sophie's story for the third time that day. I hoped it would be the last time, but I knew it wouldn't be, because I still had to tell it to my family that night. I couldn't *not* tell them.

"And," said Buddy when I'd finished, "I'm a detective and soon I'm going to be a magician." He held out the box of magic tricks. "I found them in the attic and Stacey said I could have them. I bet I can read these instructions all by myself," he added. Then he ran up to his room with his treasure.

"Mallory," said Mrs. Barrett with a huge smile, "you've worked wonders with Buddy. I'm not sure what you two have been up to, but Buddy seems much happier. We don't have battles over going to school anymore, his work has been improving, and best of all, he doesn't gag every time he hears the words 'read' or 'book.' "

I smiled back. "We tried some different things," I told Mrs. Barrett. "I mean, some unusual things. When I realized that Buddy really didn't like his workbook and reader and the flash cards, I sort of took a chance. We read comics and then we wrote our own. We read mysteries and tried to solve them. I figured it didn't matter *what* Buddy was reading as long as he *was* reading and was enjoying it.

"So when he said he wanted to read Sophie's diary, I figured, Why not? It's still reading. And you should have heard him. That diary is not easy to read — neither was the confession — but Buddy worked and worked because he wanted so badly to solve the mystery."

"Nothing like a little motivation," said Mrs. Barrett.

At that moment, Buddy came flying back down the stairs.

"Look!" he exclaimed. "I already learned one trick!"

"What, sweetie? Show us," said Mrs. Barrett immediately.

And I said, "Wait. Let's get Suzi and Marnie. You can put on a real show."

"Great!" exclaimed Buddy.

So Mrs. Barrett, Suzi, Marnie, and I squished ourselves onto the living room couch.

Buddy stood before us.

"I hold in my hand," he began, "an ordinary silk handkerchief." He waved a polka-dotted handkerchief around, I guess to prove how ordinary it was. "Now," he went on, "if someone will say the magic words — "

"I will! I will!" cried Suzi.

"Okay," replied Buddy. "Say 'abracadabra.' "

"Abracadabra," said Suzi compliantly.

Buddy pushed the handkerchief into his left hand, which he had made into a fist. When he opened his fist, the handkerchief was gone. In its place was an egg.

"Cool!" exclaimed Suzi. "How did you do that?"

"A magician," said Buddy, "never reveals his secrets."

"Well, how did you *learn* it?" asked his mother.

"Simple. I read the directions."

Mrs. Barrett and I smiled at each other over Suzi's and Marnie's heads.

And then I had to hightail it home before my parents sent the police out looking for me.

CHAPTER 15

"Guess what, guess what, guess what!" cried Stacey. She dashed into BSC headquarters ten minutes before the beginning of a Friday meeting.

"WHAT?" shouted Claudia. (Stacey had startled her. Claud was rummaging behind a chair in search of a box of Ring-Dings and hadn't heard Stacey come up the stairs.)

I was the only other club member present.

"My mom got the painting back from the art restorer today, and it — "

"Wait!" I said. "Don't say any more. Kristy'll kill us if we hear important news before she does. Can you hold off until the others arrive? Then you can tell us everything at once."

"All right," Stacey agreed, "but if I explode before five-thirty, it'll be your fault."

"I'll try to live with that," I said.

Claudia finally found the Ring-Dings and settled herself on her bed with them. "There is nothing," she said, "like a fresh, unopened package of junk food. Especially chocolate junk food. It's like holding a really huge birthday present in your lap and savoring the moments until you can open it."

Stacey rolled her eyes. Claud *did* sound a little ridiculous, but I sometimes wonder if Stacey is jealous because she can't eat things like Ring-Dings.

Claud was beginning to open the box (in that slow, careful way that some people open presents), when Kristy and Jessi arrived.

Kristy immediately plopped down in the director's chair, put on her visor, and stuck a pencil over one ear. Jessi settled herself on the floor next to me, stretching out those l-o-o-o-n-g dancer's legs of hers. We were talking about a social studies assignment we'd been given that day, when Dawn and Mary Anne arrived, grinning.

The whole club was assembled, the digital clock read 5:30 on the nose, yet nobody, not even Kristy, could ignore those grins.

"What?" said Claud excitedly. "What's going on?"

"It's our parents," said Dawn. "They called

each of us this afternoon to announce that they're going out tonight — "

"That's not unusual," Kristy interrupted.

"No," agreed Mary Anne, "but it's unusual for them to celebrate an anniversary."

"An anniversary!" I exclaimed. "What kind of anniversary?"

"They're celebrating because this is the twenty-fifth date they've been on," replied Dawn. "I mean, as adults. Not including when they were in high school."

"We figure," added Mary Anne, "that if they're counting dates and celebrating anniversaries, they must *really* be getting serious."

"Wow," said Jessi, impressed.

"I've got some news, too," spoke up Stacey.

"Ahem." Kristy tapped her pencil on Claudia's clock, indicating that it now read 5:32.

"Puh-*lease*?" said Stacey. "Remember, I said I'd burst if I don't tell this news."

"Just one thing first," replied Kristy. "Any club business?"

Well, no one was going to raise an issue if Stacey was in danger of exploding. So we all just sat there. The phone didn't ring. It wasn't even dues day.

At last Kristy said, "Okay, Stace, what's your news?"

"My mom got the painting back from the art restorer," she said in a rush, "and it's a portrait of a beautiful woman. It looks just the way Sophie described her mother's portrait in the diary. So it's *got* to be Old Hickory's daughter. . . . It's a lovely painting," she added. And then she said, "You know something? Charlotte was right. Things aren't always what they seem to be. I didn't understand what she was trying to say before, but now I see."

"Do you think Charlotte knew the portrait had been painted over?" I asked incredulously.

"Oh, no. Not at all. I think she just meant that sometimes you have to look beyond the obvious. Use your imagination, or a little ingenuity."

"Charlotte and Buddy ought to team up as detectives," I said. "They could be the next Nancy Drew and Frank Hardy."

Ring, ring.

"Ah," sighed Kristy. "I just love the first call of a meeting."

Ring, ring.

"Then answer the phone, for lord's sake," said Claud, and we all laughed.

"Hello?" said Kristy. "Baby-sitters Club. Children are our business."

(Honestly, you never know what will come out of Kristy's mouth.)

"Oh, hi, Mrs. Perkins. . . . Saturday morning? I'll see who's available and we'll get right back to you."

Before Mary Anne could even look at Saturday in the appointment pages, the phone rang again. This time it was Mrs. Arnold, needing a sitter for her twins. Then Mr. Marshall called wanting to know who was free to sit for Nina and Eleanor.

Needless to say, the next ten minutes or so were pretty busy. When things quieted down, Stacey said, "Isn't anyone curious to know what Mom and I plan to do with the portrait?"

"*I* am," I said, and the others nodded.

"Well, we thought and thought," Stacey told us, "and finally we decided to hang it in our living room over the mantelpiece. I suppose the portrait *really* belongs at the old Hickman place, since it never hung in Sophie's house, but Mom and I believe that Sophie's mother belongs with the spirits of her husband and daughter . . . I mean, if there are such things, which I doubt, but you never know."

Stacey sounded so uncertain that the rest of us couldn't help smiling.

I said, "Whether there are spirits or not, I think it's a nice idea."

"Meeee, toooo," said Kristy in her séance voice, and the seven of us nearly became hysterical. Especially when Kristy couldn't quit. "Thaaaank yoooou," she added. "You saaaaved my sooooul."

The seven of us were literally rolling with laughter (Stacey fell off the bed) when the phone rang again. Jessi composed herself first and managed to answer it — and the next job call as well.

When the appointments had been arranged, Claudia passed around the Ring-Dings. Only some of us took one. Claud did, of course, and I did because I was starving. Kristy took one, too, but Stacey and Dawn passed them up, and Jessi and Mary Anne split one. (Jessi watches her figure so she can stay in shape, and Mary Anne eats like a bird.)

"You know what I still wonder," said Kristy, after swallowing a huge mouthful of Ring-Ding.

"What?" asked Dawn.

"How Old Hickory's trunk wound up in

Sophie's attic with Sophie's things in it. Not to mention how the portrait got over there."

"Buddy and I have a theory," I spoke up.

"Oh, goody," said Kristy. She wasn't being sarcastic. She was truly interested.

"Old Hickory had given Sophie's house to his daughter, but he owned both of them — so we figured that the long-lost nephew probably inherited them both. But he only needed one house — and of course he wanted the bigger one — so maybe he started renting out the one Stacey's living in now. But not until after he moved a lot of things in the big house that he didn't want into the smaller house. I bet he just jumbled stuff up, throwing things from both places into boxes and half-empty trunks. And then maybe after awhile he sold the smaller house, forgetting about all the stuff in the attic."

"That makes sense," said Mary Anne.

"But I guess we'll never know for sure," I continued. "I mean, Buddy and I just made that up. The important thing is that we found the portrait and Jared's name has been cleared, even if it is a little late."

"Yeah," said Jessi thoughtfully. "It's too bad his name wasn't cleared while he was alive. Some things are *so* unfair."

Ring, ring.

"Yikes!" said Kristy. "What a meeting!"

Dawn answered the phone that time. Right away, she looked puzzled. Then she said, "Buddy? Is that you? . . . Sure, she's here. Hold on." Dawn handed the phone to me. "It's Buddy Barrett," she whispered, her hand over the mouthpiece. "He wants to talk to you."

"Does he sound upset?" I asked.

Dawn shook her head slowly. "No . . . more like he's excited."

I took the phone from her. "Hiya, detective," I said.

Buddy laughed. "Guess what."

"What?" I replied, wondering if Buddy was going to answer, "That's what!" which is currently Claire's favorite joke.

Instead he said, sounding extremely proud and important, "Today I was moved from the Crows to the Robins."

"Excuse me?" I replied.

"I was moved from the Crows to the Robins. The Crows are the lowest reading group in my class, and the Robins are the *middle* group."

"Oh, Buddy!" I exclaimed. "That is fabu-

142

lous. It really is! And you deserve it. You worked very hard." I cupped my hand over the receiver and relayed the news to the other BSC members.

"I bet," Buddy went on, "that I can make it into the Hawks before the school year is over. That's the highest reading group."

"I bet you can, too."

"And you know what else?"

"What?"

"I just read a *chapter* book by myself. I read the *whole* thing. And I only needed a little help from my mom."

"Fantastic! What did you read?"

"A Hardy Boys book. And I even solved the mystery before the end of the story."

Is there such a thing as too much good news? There might be. I felt a little over-whelmed after I'd hung up the phone. The portrait had been found and Buddy was becoming a reader.

"Stacey?" I said. "Is the treasury in good shape?"

"Yup," she answered. "Why?"

"Well, I was wondering. Can the treasury money pay for rewards?"

"Rewards?" Stacey glanced at Kristy. Kristy glanced at me.

"I want to reward Buddy for his hard work," I said.

"I think the treasury can handle that," replied Kristy.

"Great. There's a book I want to buy him. Anyone who likes to read *has* to read about the naughtiest kids around. So Buddy's just got to read *GOOPS and How to Be Them*."

Stacey opened the treasury envelope as carefully as if she were picking a lock. She handed me some money, grimacing.

"Bring back the change," she told me.

And we all started laughing again.

About the Author

ANN M. MARTIN did *a lot* of baby-sitting when she was growing up in Princeton, New Jersey. Now her favorite baby-sitting charge is her cat, Mouse, who lives with her in her Manhattan apartment.

Ann Martin's Apple Paperbacks are *Bummer Summer, Inside Out, Stage Fright, Me and Katie (the Pest)*, and all the other books in the Baby-sitters Club series.

She is a former editor of books for children, and was graduated from Smith College. She likes ice cream, the beach, and *I Love Lucy*; and she hates to cook.

Look for #30

MARY ANNE AND THE GREAT ROMANCE

As Dad had arranged with the maitre d',
our waiter announced that he would bring us
dessert menus, but instead he brought — a
cake! No one sang "Happy Birthday," though,
and I could tell Mrs. Schafer was relieved.

The cake was beautiful. The frosting was
white with pink and blue flowers everywhere,
and on top were four candles. We all leaned
over for a closer look, but after Mrs. Schafer
had blown out the candles, she continued to
peer at the cake.

"What is it?" asked Dawn.

Very slowly, her mother pulled out one can-
dle and held up something that had been
slipped over it onto the cake.

"Is this what I think it is?" she asked my
father.

He nodded nervously.

Mrs. Schafer held the something up for Dawn and me to see.

It was a diamond ring.

"It's — it's an engagement ring," she told us. Then she turned to Dad. "I thought we agreed — no rings. We've both been through this marriage business before. We don't need new rings."

Dad shrugged. "I just couldn't help myself," he said, "especially since I couldn't even get you a school ring back in twelfth grade."

Mrs. Schafer leaned over and kissed my father on the cheek. As you can imagine, Dawn and I just gaped at them. Finally I managed to whisper, "You mean you're getting married?"

My father and Dawn's mother nodded.

Read all the books
in the Baby-sitters Club series
by Ann M. Martin

WIN A VISIT FROM ANN M. MARTIN!

Enter THE BABY-SITTERS CLUB® Super Trivia Contest!

Which baby-sitter is Ann M. Martin's favorite? Where does she get her ideas? Get the answers to these questions and more when Ann visits your hometown and takes you and three of your friends to dinner! One lucky fan will win! Just correctly answer the questions on the coupon, and mail it by November 30, 1989.

- **2nd prize**–25 Baby-sitters Club T-shirts!
- **3rd prize**–50 pairs of Baby-sitters Club socks!

1. Monday is Dues Day for The Baby-sitters Club.   True or False

2. The Baby-sitters' favorite charge is Jenny Prezzioso.   True or False

3. There are two associate members of The Baby-sitters Club, Logan and Karen.   True or False

4. Claudia has a secret admirer on the cruise to Disney World.   True or False

Rules: Entries must be postmarked by November 30, 1989. Winners will be picked at random from all eligible entries received. No purchase necessary. Valid only in the U.S.A. Employees of Scholastic Inc., affiliates, subsidiaries, and their families not eligible. Void where prohibited. Winners will be notified by mail.

Fill in the coupon below and answer all questions. Mail to: THE BABY-SITTERS CLUB SUPER TRIVIA CONTEST, Scholastic Inc., P.O. Box 7500, 2931 E. McCarty Street, Jefferson City, MO 65102.

JOIN THE NEW BABY-SITTERS FAN CLUB!

Every Baby-sitters Fan Club member will receive: a two-year membership; an official membership card; a colorful banner; and a semi-annual newsletter with baby-sitting tips, activities and more…all for just $2.50!

No Purchase Necessary

The Baby-sitters Club Super Trivia Contest

Fill in your answers here. Indicate T for True; F for False.

1. _____   2. _____   3. _____   4. _____

Name _____ Age _____

Street _____

City, State, Zip _____

Where did you buy this Baby-sitters Club book?

- ☐ Bookstore   ☐ Drug Store
- ☐ Discount Store   ☐ Book Club
- ☐ Supermarket   ☐ Book Fair
- ☐ Other_____ specify

☐ **Yes!** Enroll me in The Baby-sitters Fan Club! I've enclosed my check or money order (no cash please) for $2.50 made payable to Scholastic Inc. at the address above.

BSC18

America's Favorite Series

THE BABY-SITTERS CLUB®

by Ann M. Martin

Collect Them All!

The seven girls at Stoneybrook Middle School get into all kinds of adventures...with school, boys, and, of course, baby-sitting!

Available wherever you buy books...or use the coupon below.

Scholastic Inc. P.O. Box 7502, 2932 E. McCarty Street, Jefferson City, MO 65102

Please send me the books I have checked above. I am enclosing $_____
(please add $1.00 to cover shipping and handling). Send check or money order—no cash or C.O.D.'s please.

Name_____

Address_____

City_____ State/Zip_____

Please allow four to six weeks for delivery. Offer good in U.S.A. only. Sorry, mail order not available to residents of Canada. Prices subject to change.